All starch and no heart . . . That's Dr Eliot
Hailey's verdict on his wife, Sister Claudia
Hailey, when they're thrown together
after a four-year separation. Having
given up hopes of a home and husband,
Claudia has dedicated herself to nursing—
but will Eliot's sudden reappearance
change her mind?

PRODIGAL DOCTOR

BY

LYNNE COLLINS

MILLS & BOON LIMITED
London · Sydney · Toronto

First published in Great Britain 1984
by Mills & Boon Limited, 15–16 Brook's Mews,
London W1A 1DR

ISBN 0 263 74811 1

Set in 10 on 11 pt Linotron Times
03–0884–55,000

Photoset by Rowland Phototypesetting Ltd
Bury St Edmunds, Suffolk
Made and printed in Great Britain by
Richard Clay (The Chaucer Press) Ltd
Bungay, Suffolk

CHAPTER ONE

THE WARD office was a sunlit oasis, a pool of quiet in the midst of activity . . . until the telephone rang. The slender girl in the dark blue dress and organza cap reached for the receiver. 'Fleming Ward. Sister speaking.' It was the expected call from an anxious relative and she was reassuring. While she talked to Mrs Hammond, she gazed through the panoramic window that overlooked the ward and watched the fluid, un-hurried movements of her capable team of nurses as they went about their routines.

It was a lovely morning, bright sunshine streaming through the tall windows to cheer the ward and the patients, and she looked with a glow of satisfaction at the double row of beds with their neat lockers and bright curtains, some pushed back and some drawn so that an injection or dressing or blanket-bath might be carried out in privacy.

Fleming was one of the busiest wards in the big teaching hospital in the heart of London that was for-mally known as The Patrick Foundation and affection-ately known to its staff and everyone else as Pat's. And Claudia Hailey was the very busy sister in charge of it.

At only twenty-four, she was young for so much responsibility but she was an excellent nurse and a good teacher and she was always quietly in control, coping with problems as they arose with the ability and confi-dence that came with years of training combined with a genuine concern for the patients. She knew just how to

5

get the best out of her nurses without working them into the ground, too.

Fleming was a busy and cheerful ward with a brisk turnover in patients and an interesting variety of surgical cases. There was a constant to and fro of visitors—consultants, registrars and their housemen, medical students, laboratory technicians and physiotherapists and social workers and a host of ancillary staff. Claudia loved nursing and she loved her ward—and Pat's was a very important part of her life. More important than anything else, in fact, taking the place of husband, home and children. She didn't expect things to change.

Now, promising to tell Mr Hammond that his wife had telephoned and sent her love, she replaced the receiver and went on with the paperwork that never seemed to lessen, bending her shining red-gold head over the desk in steady concentration. Organising ability was an essential in her job, and she'd organised to such good effect that morning that she'd found ten minutes to deal with some of the papers on her desk before the first of the surgical registrars was due on the ward for his round.

Completing the last of the discharge certificates for signature, she got up from her desk and paused by the window, glancing once more over the ward to check that all was well. A staff nurse was doing the drugs round accompanied by a junior, who was carefully checking each dosage against the chart before giving it to the patient. A houseman was setting up an intravenous drip for antibiotics for a pre-operative hernia case and using the opportunity to flirt with the first-year who was supposed to be doing the PTR round. Claudia frowned. She wasn't a martinet but she did expect her nurses to pull their weight.

The girl had transferred from Harper with only an average report on her work and she would need to do better on Fleming if she really wanted to succeed. Claudia suspected that Nurse Jilly Wayne was more interested in marriage than medicine and regarded Pat's as a hunting-ground for a husband. Flirtation was rife, for all Matron's efforts to stamp it out, and where an affair didn't actually exist the grapevine was always willing to invent one, Claudia thought dryly. She was careful not to give it any ammunition—and anyway, she was much too busy to have time for flirtation.

She watched Mr Duckworth making his way along the ward in shabby slippers and plaid dressing-gown, newspaper beneath his arm. He was getting over an operation to remove crushed spinal discs and walking was a slow and painful business. He was on his way to discuss the day's racing tips with another patient. Mr Potter was going to theatre later that day and he'd be glad of something else to think about until his anxiety began to dissolve with the administration of the pre-med injection.

Mr Clements was sitting up and taking notice this morning, she observed . . . particular notice of one of her nurses, in fact. Men responded readily to Carol Gray's pretty face and bright smile and she was a tonic on the ward, although Claudia frequently doubted that the accident-prone junior would ever make a qualified nurse.

The swing of the ward doors attracted her attention. The flash of a white coat and the gleam of a blond head told her that Trevor Page, registrar to Professor Harding, had entered the ward. She'd been waiting for him. Now, she felt a slight and rather foolish reluctance to leave the peace of her office and join him on the round of his patients.

She was always so carefully in control of her emotions that it was disturbing to realise that she'd weakened where the good-looking and very popular surgeon was concerned. Liking him, she'd shown it to some extent since they'd been working together on the ward and they'd become friends. But only during working hours, safely within the hospital walls. Claudia kept her off-duty life firmly separate from her job as ward sister at Pat's.

'Excuse me, Sister . . .' A junior paused by the open door of the office. 'Are you busy? Staff Nurse Gordon wants to know if she should accompany Mr Page on his round this morning.'

Claudia hesitated, tempted to plead pressure of paperwork and gratify the optimism of her senior staff nurse who'd welcome an opportunity for a few minutes with the surgeon she fancied. But it wasn't part of her job to encourage any kind of involvement between doctors and nurses on the ward and she had no reason to avoid meeting Trevor, she told herself firmly. 'I'm just coming,' she said briskly. 'Thank you, Nurse.' But she didn't immediately move from her vantage point at the window, observing the surgeon as he talked to Julie Gordon.

A clever and caring surgeon, he was a favourite with patients and staff. He was also very good-looking with his blond hair and dancing blue eyes and the smile that flurried the hearts of her junior nurses. And her own, just a little, Claudia admitted frankly. But there was no future in liking him or encouraging his interest. Past experience had proved the folly of caring and giving too much to a man, she reminded herself. She'd been badly hurt and she didn't mean to be hurt again. Only a fool invited heartache and humiliation for a second time . . .

Thrusting personal thoughts and feelings to the back of her mind, something that came easily after years of practice, Claudia hurried into the ward to break some bad news to the surgeon. Earlier that day, two of his patients had died. One of them had been inevitable and expected daily since a laparotomy had revealed an inoperable tumour. But the other, an eighteen-year-old student stabbed in a street fight, had been unexpected and distressing.

As duty surgeon, Trevor had been called late at night to operate on the youth and he'd worked for two hours to stem internal bleeding and repair a jagged tear in the peritoneum. The prognosis had been optimistic when the patient was transferred from intensive care to Fleming, but he'd gone into cardiac arrest in the early hours and the emergency team had failed to rescuscitate him.

Claudia told him about the boy first. Dismay touched the blue eyes. Then he balled a fist and slammed it hard into the palm of the other hand in sudden, angry frustration. 'That's damnable!' It was explosive. 'Such a bloody waste!'

Claudia sympathised. They all hated to lose a patient. Surgeons like Trevor felt it as a personal blow when someone that they'd worked hard to keep alive died in defiance of all their efforts and normal expectation.

'I'm afraid that Mr Bennett has gone, too,' she said quietly but brisk, unemotional. She wasn't uncaring. But a nurse had to acquire a second skin in the early days of her training if she was to survive the trauma and tragedy of working for her state registered badge.

He nodded acceptance. 'Eighty-eight, wasn't he? That lad was just eighteen. Robbed of perhaps seventy good years because of an argument that got out of hand.' He sighed and ran a hand through the thick blond hair. 'What about the parents, Sister?'

'They're here. In my sitting-room. Very shocked, of

course. I've given them some tea and left them to comfort each other.'

'Would you like me to talk to them?'

Knowing the sureness of his touch, Claudia agreed and took him along to her sitting-room. The mother was naturally inconsolable, a damp bundle of trembling misery. The father was tight-lipped, silent, bottling his feelings. Jamie had been their only child, a good boy, never in any trouble and doing well at college. Now, he was suddenly and quite unbelievably dead. The light of their life, snuffed out like a candle.

Trevor knew just what to say and do to comfort and reassure the shocked and bewildered couple and it wasn't just the glibness of long experience in such matters. No one in the profession ever really became inured or hardened to dealing with the bereaved.

With an arm about the mother's shaking shoulders and a warm sympathy of manner that encouraged the father to spill some of his grief and bitter anger, he might have been a friend or a member of the family, Claudia felt as she left them together for a few minutes. That was the secret of his success as a surgeon and his popularity as a person, she decided. He really cared about people rather than conventions or medical etiquette. Or his ego, she thought, remembering a very different man who'd had a high opinion of his abilities and a selfish tendency to put himself and his needs before everyone and everything else.

Whisking her thoughts from a forbidden path, she went back to the ward to talk to the clerk about the day's new admissions who would shortly be brought up from reception.

'Three today, isn't it?' she asked, putting her hand on the pile of new folders.

'That's right. Two hernias and a mastoidectomy. The

last one's only twelve but there isn't a bed for him in children's surgical at the moment. He needs urgent surgery so they've sent him to us, he'll probably be moved in a few days.'

'Before he gets too lively, I hope. Twelve-year-old boys can cause mayhem and we're much too busy to cope with that on top of everything else,' Claudia said firmly.

Sally Hayes smiled. 'I'll keep an eye on the situation.'

'Two hernias.' Claudia skimmed lightly through the first of the files. 'Nice, straightforward cases that shouldn't present any problems. This one . . . Mr Greene—he's one of Professor Harding's patients, I see. Mr Page is on the ward at the moment and may want to examine him before he leaves, so we shall have to hustle him into bed as soon as he comes up from reception.' She looked along the ward to the empty beds that awaited their new occupants. 'Let me know as soon as he arrives.'

'Yes, of course, Sister.'

'I'll try to be on hand to deal with the little boy. He's bound to be bewildered and I expect his ear is very painful.' Claudia turned as Trevor came into the ward and beckoned to the junior who was in charge of the trolley that was stacked with the patients' files.

She accompanied the surgeon on his round with a cool impersonality of manner that didn't betray the growing warmth in her liking for him. She was always very careful in her dealings with the registrars or housemen, for the juniors were much too ready to exaggerate the merest exchange of smiles or any remark not connected with a patient's treatment or progress into a budding romance between doctor and nurse. Pat's was a hotbed of gossip—like any place where men and women worked in close proximity.

Trevor liked to take his time over the round even when he was due in theatre. He liked his patients to feel that there was plenty of time to air anxiety, to ask questions or to detail their symptoms. He was informal, interested, subtly reassuring. He was trusted by his patients, admired by theatre and ward staff and respected by the students, who learned far more from him than surgical techniques and procedures.

The round was a lengthy one and took up far too much of Claudia's valuable time. The junior was looking anguished, too. Recalling her own first-year days when there had been a hundred and one chores and never enough time, Claudia released her to get on with her routines and took charge of the trolley with its neat stack of files.

As they walked towards the next patient, Trevor said lightly, 'You must have a great deal to do, Sister. If you want to get on with something else, I can manage for myself, you know.'

It was a thoughtful suggestion but out of the question, of course. For the Patrick Foundation rigidly maintained all the old traditions and deplored the falling standards of other hospitals that had adopted the national uniform and where doctors and students wandered in and out of wards as they pleased and sisters were more involved with administration and form-filling than with their patients. Pat's was old-fashioned and proud of it!

Claudia wondered if she'd betrayed her impatience. 'A well-run ward runs itself, Mr Page,' she told him briskly, consciously quoting the maxim of an elderly predecessor who'd run her ward and ruled both nurses and patients with an iron hand and as much starch in her attitude as in her fluted organza cap.

The surgeon smiled, eyes crinkling with amusement. 'An admirable sentiment. I wonder why it should convey a mental picture of Sister sailing placidly through the ward while the juniors panic behind the scenes or sob their hearts out in the sluice?'

'I hope my juniors know better than to indulge in panic on my ward,' she said, mock-stern, the hint of a smile in her own eyes. 'They may do as they please in their own time, of course.'

'Martinet,' he reproached, teasing.

The warmth of his smile was reflected in the blue eyes and Claudia's heart unexpectedly bumped in her breast—the very heart that thought it had forgotten how to respond to a certain glow in a man's eyes. Halting the trolley, she began to riffle busily and unnecessarily through the files. The one she wanted was to hand and easily recognisable but she needed a moment or two to master the absurd fancy that she was falling in love with the blond surgeon. Such nonsense! She knew all about loving—only too well! She didn't mean to repeat such a painful and disappointing experience.

Trevor smiled at his patient. 'How are you this morning, Mr Lambert? Any pain? Eating well? Let's have a look at my handiwork, Sister.'

Claudia drew down the bedclothes and smiled reassuringly as she unbuttoned the patient's pyjama jacket and removed a dry dressing to reveal the nicely healing cicatrice of a cholecystectomy. The old man studied the surgeon anxiously as he glanced through the file and then laid it on the locker. Trevor began to probe the wound with clever, sensitive hands, eyes intent on the patient's face for the least change of expression that might indicate pain or tenderness beyond the norm.

'I'll have a look at the chart, Sister.' She handed it to him and he glanced over it carefully and then nodded, satisfied. 'You seem to be my star patient, Mr

Lambert,' he approved, bringing a gleam of relief to blue eyes that were misted by cataracts. 'We'll be sending you home very soon.'

Observing a flicker of dismay, he lingered to help the fumbling, arthritic hands with buttons and encouraged a rambling recital of domestic problems. Then, patting the thin shoulder, he promised that something should be done to iron them out before the old man was discharged.

Claudia knew that he'd make a point of contacting the welfare officer who liaised between patients in hospital and in their own homes. She returned Mr Lambert's chart to its hook and his file to the trolley, having tidied the bed, plumped the pillows, poured fresh water from the jug on the locker and returned newspapers and reading glasses to the old man in one seemingly continuous and smoothly unobtrusive movement.

It was such thoughtful, unasked attention to the comfort and convenience of her patients, carried out so quietly that it almost went unnoticed, that made her such a good nurse and had won her promotion to ward sister at an unusually early age. Trevor admired the professionalism that she combined with a warmly personal touch. As well as liking and the throb of physical attraction, he admired her tremendously.

He'd joined Professor Harding's team as surgical registrar in the same week that Claudia Hailey had become Sister in charge of Fleming. Knowing little about her, he'd been surprised by the youth and striking good looks of the girl in the navy blue dress with gleaming red-gold hair neatly coiled beneath the fluted cap that was worn so proudly by Pat's sisters. He was impressed by her cool and unhurried competence, her tactful handling of nurses and ward staff, the warm and cheerful sympathy and concern for her patients and the ease with which she'd apparently slipped into her new role without even a hiccup.

Surgical wards were always busy and very demanding, a challenge even for a nurse of long experience. Claudia was all nurse, caring and responsible and efficient. At the same time, she was all woman. The patients brightened when she walked into the ward and sometimes seemed to get well against all the odds because she rallied them with the right word at the right moment.

Her nurses worked well under her quiet and capable direction and they liked her cheerful readiness to roll up her sleeves and tackle any chore when they were really rushed. The crustiest of consultants smiled approval on the youthful Sister Hailey and she could instil confidence in the rawest of medical students by leaving him to examine a patient and take copious notes at his leisure, instead of hovering critically and complaining of upset routines as some sisters did.

Trevor had worked at Pat's for three years but their paths hadn't crossed until his new job took him regularly to Fleming. It was a big hospital with many wards and departments and there were so many nurses about the place that it was easy to overlook one who was so determined to blend with her surroundings. Even one as distinctive and attractive as Claudia, with her lovely hair and unusual eyes and the sweet smile that brought an unexpected beauty to the oval face with its rather grave expression.

In six months of working together, he'd never known her impatient or irritable or even frayed at the edges, despite the demands and difficulties of her job. She was a really nice girl, so it was surprising that the grapevine never seemed to link her name with any man at Pat's—or outside it. Over the months, Trevor's interest and affection had grown steadily. Rather too used to the impact of his blond good looks and personable charm on most women, he was intrigued by the cool friendliness that was not at all encouraging. If she was pleased by his persistent pursuit, she wasn't showing it, he thought wryly. He was curious to know if it was all men or just doctors that she kept so firmly at bay.

The round finally over, they walked together through the swing-doors of the ward. He was destined for theatre and a long day of operating. Claudia was *en route* to her office.

The corridor was quiet, deserted. Trevor paused, checking her with a hand on her arm, smiling down at her. 'I've seats for the new musical at the Pantheon,' he told her, taking prompt advantage of the fact that for once there was neither nurse nor ward-maid within sight and sound. 'I'd like to take you to see it, Claudia. We could have a drink before the show and a late supper afterwards. We can't go on meeting like this, you know,' he added.

Claudia was surprised to discover that she was rather tempted by the invitation. Resolutely, she shook her head. 'Sounds lovely, but I'm afraid I can't make it.'

He didn't point out that he hadn't specified any particular evening. 'You turn me down with monotonous regularity,' he said wryly. 'I guess I'm a fool to keep trying.'

'I'm flattered that you want to take me out,' she assured him lightly.

'But just not interested.' He looked down at her steadily. 'I'm falling in love with you, Claudia. But I guess you know that.'

Her heart jolted. But she knew better than to be seduced by meaningless words from a charmer. She wasn't a green girl. 'Don't do that,' she said brightly, refusing to take him seriously. 'It won't get you anywhere, I'm afraid. The chemistry is lacking.' It wasn't strictly true. But she couldn't tell him the real reason why she kept him and every other man at a safe distance. Keeping her secrets had become a habit.

Trevor frowned. 'You just won't give the chemistry a chance,' he declared with some exasperation. '*Keep off* is written all over you!'

'Trevor, I'm a sister. You're a registrar. We can't afford to get involved with each other,' she said firmly, fighting an absurd inclination to do so for all her resolution. He was such a nice man. 'It isn't wise or practical. Emotions get in the wrong way at the wrong times and demands are made that can't be met. Too many people take an interest and the relationship inevitably suffers. We're good friends, I hope. Please, let's keep it that way!'

Sensitive to a hint of tension and a wealth of feeling behind the quiet words that made him wonder, he chose to lighten the moment. 'I shall probably go into a decline,' he warned cheerfully. 'I'm not used to disappointment in love.'

Claudia relaxed, smiled. 'I can assure you that it isn't fatal.' After all, *she* had survived, she thought—but only just, and she didn't mean to make the same mistake again. So she resisted and even rather resented the surgeon's persistent little tug at her heart.

He left her, hands thrusting almost angrily into the pockets of his white coat and a slightly downcast slump to the broad shoulders. Then, hardening a heart that seemed inclined to be much too foolish where he was concerned, Claudia turned away. Day-dreaming about a good-looking surgeon wouldn't lessen the pile of papers on her desk or write Matron's report, she reminded herself firmly.

Someone was waiting in her office. A man who stood

at the panoramic window, surveying the ward, his back to her as Claudia paused at the open door. Very tall, dark-haired, lean and lithe and long-limbed, his relaxed attitude conveying confidence as well as an easy familiarity with the hospital surroundings. Claudia wondered if he was a doctor minus his white coat. Then she supposed him to be a new patient or a relative and wondered why he'd been shown into her office to wait without her knowledge. She prepared to slip into her role of ward sister. Suddenly, shocked, she realised that she knew the set of that proud, dark head, the confident stance of that lean figure and the very physical magnetism that seemed to emanate from the visitor.

Her heart almost stopped as he turned, smiling.

'Sister Hailey, I presume?' he said, enjoying her astonishment and dismay. Deep-set, dark eyes regarded her with mocking amusement and a great deal of self-assurance.

Claudia closed the door, struggling to maintain her composure, wondering if she was hallucinating or if it really was her long-lost husband.

Out of the blue. Without a word of warning.

Smiling at her just as though it was four hours rather than four years since they'd last met . . .

CHAPTER TWO

CLAUDIA had always believed that if, by some miracle, Eliot should turn up again one day in just this totally unexpected fashion, she'd hurl herself into his arms on a sob of delight and thankfulness. For wouldn't it be a dream come true?

But now that it had actually happened and he was standing in front of her, smiling at her so confidently, she didn't feel the slightest inclination to do anything of the kind. After that initial moment of stunned astonishment and disbelief, she didn't feel anything at all as she looked at the man who'd hurt and humiliated her and finally walked out on her four years earlier.

It was hard to believe that this was the man she'd gone on loving despite everything. In her mind's eye, he'd been something really special. In reality, he was just another man, after all. With more than his share of good looks and with a kind of charisma that had first attracted her—and too many other women for her peace of mind. But just a man like any other.

Nevertheless, she moved behind the barricade of her desk and sat down, regarding him coolly and without emotion. She reached for a file from the neat pile by her hand and placed it in front of her on the desk, carefully, as if to imply that her work was much more important than an unexpected and inconvenient visit from an estranged husband.

Eliot's smile deepened. She was every inch the efficient nurse, the competent ward sister, and he was more impressed by the composure and the newfound

19

confidence than he meant her to know. She was even lovelier than he'd remembered, too.

No wonder he'd rushed into that disastrous and short-lived marriage, briefly enchanted by her good looks and superb figure and her eager, glowing love for him. What man could have resisted so much temptation? Claudia had been the kind to hold out for marriage and he'd been willing enough. How could he or any man have known that she would be such a disappointment?

'Am I such a stranger?' he asked, amused, eyes dancing with a little gleam of mockery. 'Don't I merit even one kiss of welcome?'

Claudia didn't rise to the bait. She picked up her pen, uncapped it, poised to write. 'What are you doing here? What do you want, Eliot?' It was cool, light and very nearly indifferent.

There ought to be a wild tumult of emotion in her heart and mind instead of this calm acceptance. There ought to be a dream-like quality about this meeting with him after so long. But she merely felt a mild irritation that he'd chosen to walk back into her life on such a busy morning. It was typically Eliot!

He perched confidently on a corner of the desk. 'At the moment, I'm admiring all that you've achieved,' he told her. 'But I always knew that you'd make a career out of nursing if I wasn't around to get in the way. It was always more important to you than anything else.'

She sent him a long, level look. 'No, Eliot. It *became* more important than anything else. You didn't leave me with much of an alternative to a nursing career.'

He shrugged, unabashed. 'Neither of us was ready for marriage. We were just a couple of kids, Claudia. Impulsive, irresponsible, immature. If we'd gone to bed together a few times instead of rushing to the altar we might both have been spared a lot of heartache.'

'Is that a preliminary to a suggestion of divorce?'

He raised an eyebrow at her bluntness. 'Not necessarily. Is that the way it sounds?'

'I can't think of any other reason why you should suddenly want to see me.' She glanced pointedly at her watch. 'It isn't very convenient timing. I'm very busy.'

'Too busy to be interested in the man you married? Don't you want to know how I've been and what I've been doing with my life all these years?'

'Not particularly. I don't know that I'm interested, frankly. It's water under the bridge, isn't it? Just like our marriage.' She smiled coolly, rather surprised by the detachment she felt—and glad of it. She'd always believed that pride could have no place in her heart where he was concerned. Now she knew that she'd have despised herself if she'd fallen into his arms after years of neglect and callous indifference. 'You wiped that clean off the slate. And me, too. Did you ever wonder how *I* was or what I was doing?'

'I wondered why you never cashed any of the cheques I sent you,' he admitted.

'I didn't need the money.' She'd needed him, she thought with a sudden welling of bitterness. How could he have been so insensitive as to suppose that money was an acceptable substitute? She'd seen those regular monthly cheques as an added humiliation, a renewal of her hurt, and torn them up. But when they eventually stopped coming she'd felt their absence as the snapping of the last link in their unsatisfactory relationship.

'No, I guess not.' A wry smile tugged at his lips. 'Ran home to Daddy, did you? And he gladly went back to paying the bills, no doubt. There was no longer any need for all that independence when I wasn't around to fight with you over it, of course. It isn't surprising that we didn't work out, is it? A girl with your background and a struggling young doctor. We had nothing in common.'

'I thought we had love in common,' Claudia reminded him.

'Unfortunately, you didn't know the meaning of the word, my dear.' It was blunt, scathing.

Her eyes sparked at the injustice of the words. 'I know what *you* meant by it!' She lifted the receiver as the telephone rang, thankful for the interruption. This wasn't the time or the place to quarrel with him. 'Fleming Ward, Sister Hailey speaking . . .'

While Claudia dealt with the query from the pathology department, she regarded Eliot thoughtfully, dispassionately. He'd matured, of course—and rather more than one would expect after a mere four years of absence. He was even more attractive these days, she admitted. His handsome face was lean and intelligent and deeply tanned and there was the hint of humour in the set of his mobile mouth and the way that his deepset, dark eyes crinkled at the corners.

He seemed entirely at his ease as he sat on a corner of her desk, swinging a long leg, turning the pages of a medical journal that she hadn't yet found time to read and listening with half an ear to her conversation. But her experienced eye observed signs of tension. The nerve that throbbed in his jaw, for instance—and the long fingers that beat a silent tattoo on her desk.

He was thinner than he ought to be and she noted a few silver strands among the crisp waves and curls of his gleaming black hair. There was something else, too. Something that she couldn't exactly define but which instinct and her training both recognised. She was looking at a man who'd recently been very ill, she decided.

He wore a light-weight tan suit with cream shirt, striped tie and tan shoes and his hair had been carefully brushed. The formal clothes and well-groomed appearance implied that he'd taken pains. For a special appointment—or to come looking for her? He still wore his hair slightly too long, the tight black curls on the nape of his neck inviting a woman's fingers to twine and tug.

He'd always been attractive to women, of course. Too attractive. He'd always been totally self-assured, too. But he'd lost a lot of his exuberance and the easy charm that had endeared him so swiftly to the girl she'd been when they first met. Then he'd been little more than a boy. Now he was very much a man, Claudia thought.

As she replaced the receiver, he looked up from *The Lancet*. Their eyes met and held for a moment and Claudia was thankful to find that the slight gleam in the depths of his didn't have the least impact on her heart. She really was over him at last. But it was still a shock to realise that she'd fallen out of love without knowing it. Even if her recovery had been long overdue . . .

'You've been ill, haven't you?' she asked quietly.

He inclined his head, smiling. 'Perceptive, aren't you?' he drawled.

Claudia shrugged. 'I *am* a nurse.' She hesitated and then said with the politeness of a stranger, 'I hope it wasn't anything serious.'

'Just a touch of fever that I picked up in Tanzania.'

She wondered if his tone was slightly too dismissive and if a visit to a specialist explained his presence at the hospital. 'Tanzania? Were you there on holiday?' It was poignant to realise how little she knew about him and his movements of the past four years.

'Not exactly. I've been working at a medical mission for three years. Heat, flies, smells and the unequal struggle with poverty and disease finally defeated me, I'm afraid. I never did have much staying-power, you'll recall,' he added mockingly.

'Three years is a long time.' Claudia looked at him with some curiosity and a flicker of new respect. 'It obviously suited you more than marriage. But I wouldn't have thought that kind of life was your style.'

'I didn't go out there to enjoy myself, Claudia. I needed the experience and the chance of some useful research. It's paid off, I'm pleased to say. I've just landed the job of senior medical registrar to Sir Hartley Oates.' He named one of Pat's leading consultants in child care with obvious satisfaction.

'Congratulations,' Claudia said evenly. If it had happened sooner she might have been thrilled and thankful that circumstances had brought him back into her life, and even optimistic about the chances of patching up their broken marriage. Somehow, she could only feel a kind of resentment that he'd turned up again just as she'd got used to being without him—had begun to feel that loving him belonged to the past and that there might be a future for her with someone else. Someone like Trevor Page, for instance.

'I don't feel that you're pleased,' he said lightly, observing the play of expression across her good-looking face and recognising a hint of dismay in the striking amber eyes.

'I don't feel that it concerns me, to be frank,' she returned bluntly. 'We've led our own lives for years and proved that we don't need each other. Anything that happens to you no longer affects me.' It was cool, decisive.

'You've become very hard, Claudia. Did I do that to you?' He reached a hand across the expanse of desk to touch her cheek in a gesture that was almost a caress, almost an act of contrition.

Claudia moved her face from the touch that no longer had the power to stir her heart. He felt like a stranger.

He certainly didn't seem like the man she'd once married, the man she'd loved so much, the man she'd missed and yearned for throughout the long and lonely years.

She looked at him levelly. 'I had to grow up in a hurry, Eliot. You were going to love me and look after me for the rest of my life. Suddenly you weren't around any more and I had to get on with looking after myself,' she said without self-pity, without reproach, simply stating facts. 'Picking up the pieces, starting over, forgetting . . . it wasn't easy and I daresay I grew hard in the process.'

'And have you forgotten?' He smiled but the dark eyes were intent, narrowed.

'I certainly haven't forgiven!' It was quick and angry. 'If you expected me to throw my arms about you and cry welcome then you're disappointed, I'm afraid!'

He laughed, soft and slightly mocking. 'My dear girl, I didn't give you a thought. I never expected to see you, in fact. I'd no idea that you still worked here, let alone had reached the dizzy heights of ward sister. Quite by chance, someone mentioned my namesake on the staff—Sister Hailey, Claudia Hailey—and asked if we were related. I couldn't doubt that it was you, of course, but it didn't seem possible that you were a sister when you were only a student nurse when we last saw each other. You've really done remarkably well, you know.' It was genuine admiration. As a doctor, he knew just how hard she must have worked and how dedicated she must have been to attain her sister's strings at such an early age.

Claudia ignored the commendation. 'So you explained that I was your wife.' The light tone strove to conceal an instinctive and very natural dismay. She'd kept her secret for too long to want it carelessly exposed by a chance exchange between doctors.

'I said that there was a connection of sorts and left it at that.' He glanced at her bare left hand, lying on the desk between them. 'It seems I did the right thing. As you don't wear your wedding-ring, I take it that you don't wish to advertise the fact that you have a husband.'

'It saves a lot of explanations.'

He nodded, understanding. 'While there have been several occasions when I've found it extremely convenient to explain that I already have a wife,' he said with a hint of devilment.

'I can believe that.' Her lip curled with scorn and the ice that tinkled in her tone forewarned him that she had no desire to hear anything about his amorous exploits of the past four years.

Eliot laughed. 'Anyway, I felt that I couldn't leave this morning without making the effort to see you, if only for a few moments.'

'For the sake of auld lang syne, no doubt,' she suggested sardonically, unmoved by the smile he bestowed on her—although it did remind her painfully of the engaging young doctor she'd found so irresistible and so endearing when she was a second-year nurse with a foolish readiness to part with her heart.

'For the sake of satisfying my curiosity, actually,' he commented. 'I've often wondered what it was about you that made me feel I had to marry you. I've never felt that strongly about any other woman, before or since. Now, I think I know. Seeing you just now,' he indicated the observation panel that had enabled him to study her while she moved about the ward, instructing her nurses, attending to patients, accompanying a doctor on his round, 'I almost didn't recognise you. You've become a beautiful woman as well as a competent ward sister while my back's been turned. I'm really very proud of my wife.'

The surprising words held the ring of sincerity and the warm glow in the dark eyes spoke volumes. Claudia wasn't impressed and she didn't mean to be swayed by sentiment at this late stage in their relationship. He'd swept her into loving and marrying him with that glib tongue and dangerous charm and she'd paid the penalty for trusting him with her heart and her happiness. She wouldn't allow him to sweep back into her life all in a moment—if that was what he had in mind, she decided firmly. There were all the signs of it in the way he looked and spoke, she felt, utterly astonished. It was a dream come true—much too late!

Eliot rose abruptly from the desk, sensing that she was near to sending him away with a brisk reminder that she had claims on her time and attention that she couldn't continue to ignore. 'You won't believe that I've thought about you, very often. Even missed you, on occasions. But it happens to be true,' he said lightly. 'We had our problems and not enough patience or know-how—or love—to sort them out. You failed me and I hurt you, and we were obviously better off apart. We were both too young for marriage, of course. Now—well, things might be very different if we were meeting for the first time at this moment. We might feel that we had a lot to give each other . . .'

The door opened with a rush and no warning knock and an agitated first-year nurse paused on the threshold, flushed and breathless. Eliot glowered and Claudia raised a disapproving eyebrow at the stained apron and fly-away cap.

'Well, what is it, Nurse?' she prompted as the girl stood silent and unnerved, baby-blue eyes filling with tears. 'What have you done this time?' Her tone was resigned. She was used to Carol Gray's disasters, which ranged so far from a broken thermometer to crashing a loaded trolley at the feet of a startled consultant.

'Oh, Sister!' It was a strangled gasp. 'I'm sorry, Sister, but I've pulled out Mr Nunn's drainage tube and he's in a dreadful state and I don't know what to do and Staff Nurse Gordon is busy with Mr Swann's round and Staff Nurse Wilmot's gone to early lunch and . . .'

'Very well, Nurse. I'll be there in a moment,' Claudia broke into the almost incoherent gabble, stifling a sigh and a sharp declaration that the girl would never make a nurse. She'd known many a clumsy and careless first-year turn into an excellent nurse once she'd mastered the fear of doing something utterly dreadful to an unsuspecting patient.

'Change that apron and then go back to Mr Nunn and reassure the poor man. I know it's alarming, but it's easily done and easily put right as long as you keep your head. I'll show you what to do so that you'll know if it ever happens again. Off you go.' As the junior scurried away, she got to her feet. 'I'm sorry, Eliot. But you can see that I'm much too busy to hold a post-mortem on a dead marriage,' she said briskly, her smile skating over him without warmth.

'A dead marriage ought to be decently buried,' he said smoothly. 'Why haven't you divorced me, Claudia? You had good reason and sufficient grounds. Don't you want to be free?'

She moved purposefully towards the door. 'I'm just as free as I need to be. There's no other man that I'm anxious to marry, if that's what you're really asking,' she said dryly.

'I couldn't complain if there'd been a dozen men since I left you.' Eliot followed her into the corridor and fell into step at her side as she headed for the ward.

'No, you couldn't complain,' she agreed tartly. 'But I've been more interested in my job than looking for another husband who might be just as unsatisfactory as you were.' She said it to hurt, still smarting from the blunt accusation that she'd failed him. As she remembered, it was the other way round!

He detained her briefly with a hand on her arm when they reached the swing-doors. 'Meet me later. We'll have lunch.' It wasn't an invitation or a request.

Claudia stiffened at the crisp, authoritative tone. 'I don't think . . .'

He didn't allow her to continue. 'Even sisters have to eat and we need to talk. Sort things out. Meet me in the Plough at one o'clock. For the sake of auld lang syne,' he added sardonically in his turn.

He moved away as the first-year hurried up in a clean apron, cap carefully adjusted on her fair curls. Claudia observed the way that his glance swept comprehensively and with male interest over the girl's trim figure and pretty face. He hadn't changed. But *she* had. For she didn't feel even the smallest twinge of jealousy at that obvious gleam of admiration for another woman in the dark eyes.

She looked after him, marvelling that she'd once admired that arrogance and submitted to it readily, and now found it intensely irritating. He hadn't given her time to argue, to refuse. He knew that she'd meet him, too. Not because she wished to pick up former threads but because, as he'd said, it was time they straightened out their lives. She'd been living in limbo long enough.

'Sister?' Carol Gray prompted her, anxiously, convinced that a patient was at death's door because of her clumsiness.

Claudia smiled at her, sensitive to the girl's anxiety and remembering her own first-year horrors. 'Yes, of course, Mr Nunn. Let's go and make him comfortable again.'

But while she showed how to replace the drainage tube and how to restore the patient's confidence as well as his comfort, she found that her thoughts persistently turned to Eliot.

Had her love really died so completely or was the numbness of her feelings only reaction to the shock of seeing him again after so long? She'd loved him so much. She'd gone on loving despite the hurt and humiliation and hopelessness of their brief marriage. So she was shocked by the thought that her loyal heart had tired of loving when she'd been so sure that he was the only man for her, for ever. Even though he wasn't and never had been worth it.

She had just finished her first year at Pat's when she was tumbled into love and rushed into marriage by Eliot, the good-looking young doctor from Central, met at a rugger-club dance after a match between the two hospitals.

Newly qualified and 'walking the wards' for the obligatory year, Eliot couldn't really afford a wife as well as the expenses of running a home. He'd encouraged her to carry on with her training and she'd been given permission to live out. Although their marriage had been generally known at the time, it had created little interest and she'd been grateful for that when it all fell apart.

Claudia had tried hard to be the kind of wife that he wanted while coping with the demands of second-year nursing, but he made few allowances and many criticisms. He, too, was beset by the long hours, perpetual weariness and chronic anxieties of his own job. Their hours of duty seldom seemed to coincide and the little time they had together seemed to be made up of snatched lovemaking and hurried meals and arguments about money.

Eliot couldn't, or wouldn't, understand her reluctance to ask her famous and wealthy parents for the financial help that she knew would be given gladly with no questions asked. In fact, she'd been much too proud to admit that they had any problems when they'd married—much against the concerned and well-meaning advice of family and friends. Head over heels in love, they couldn't wait to be married and they'd been so sure that they could overcome any problems. So no one had been allowed to know that they weren't both as happy and confident about the future as they'd expected to be.

Things had gone from bad to worse as Eliot fell out of love as easily as he'd fallen into it. As the weeks passed, Claudia saw less and less of him and chose to believe the casual excuses that he offered, closing her mind to the small evidences that he was unfaithful to her. Proud and naturally reserved, she hadn't talked about her failing marriage to anyone and it had limped along for a few more months while she went on loving and hoping. But Eliot had finally admitted that there was someone else and Claudia had been forced to realise the futility of clinging to a man who no longer wanted her. But she hadn't been able to stop loving.

Pat's had been her salvation and her sanctuary in the difficult months that followed. She'd thrown herself heart and soul into nursing. None of her colleagues now remembered or cared that she'd married a doctor from Central. She didn't wear her wedding-ring and she maintained a careful gulf between two separate worlds.

Now, with Eliot appointed to a post at Pat's by an ironic twist of fate, the grapevine would soon be humming with the news, she thought bitterly. For how could she hope to keep it a secret that the new medical registrar was her husband?

CHAPTER THREE

IT WAS a few minutes before one-thirty when Claudia emerged into the bright sunshine of the day, having left her senior staff nurse in capable charge of the ward until her return at four o'clock. She paused for a moment at the head of the wide stone steps outside the main entrance, scanning the pavements, unconsciously attracting attention from the steady stream of patients and relatives and staff who were entering and leaving the famous and always busy hospital.

There was something particularly striking about the slender girl with her gleaming hair and classic good looks and the air of withdrawal that she wrapped about her like the cloak she was wearing over her navy blue dress. She descended the steps and crossed the main road to the pub that Eliot had named as their meeting-place, wondering if he had deliberately and rather cruelly chosen a venue that would revive memories of their brief and frenetic courtship.

The Plough was a favourite haunt of Pat's staff and it would be crowded at this hour with doctors and medical students and off-duty nurses as well as ancillary staff. Claudia knew that as a ward sister she must be a familiar figure to most of them and she didn't doubt that there would be speculation if she was seen with a very attractive and undeniably distinctive man. The first of the rumours were sure to be flying about Pat's by the end of the day, she thought ruefully.

She pushed through swing-doors into the saloon bar, disliking the smell of beer that instantly assailed her nose

32

and the hubbub that pounded her ears and the stuffiness of the place on such a warm day. She looked around for Eliot but couldn't see him among the crush of people at the bar and reminded herself that she was slightly early—and that punctuality had never been one of his strong points.

She stood still, hesitant and rather nervous, feeling that all eyes were on her for at the best of times she had a particular dislike of entering a pub by herself. Then she caught sight of a familiar blond head and on a sudden impulse, she made her way through the crowd to Trevor Page's side.

He smiled down at her in surprise and warm welcome as she touched his arm and said his name with a hint of friendliness. 'Driven to drink by the demands of the job at last?' he suggested, teasing. 'I knew you'd crack one day. What can I get you, Claudia?'

'Nothing, thanks. I'm not drinking. I'm just looking for someone . . . for a friend,' she qualified, with a tinge of embarrassment.

'Will I do?' Trevor smiled into the amber eyes. For once they weren't so carefully cool and reluctant to commit her to anything more than the casual camaraderie that existed between senior staff at Pat's and didn't always extend beyond the hospital walls. 'I'm a friend,' he added, the glow in his eyes implying his longing to be very much more. He was encouraged that she'd sought him out, for he'd almost despaired of melting the ice that seemed to surround her heart.

'Yes, I know.' Claudia smiled at him, reassured by the sincerity of his tone and glad that he wasn't bearing a grudge because she'd turned him down earlier that day. 'Another time, perhaps!'

'I'll hold you to that,' he said quickly.

She laughed, but she was woman enough to be pleased

and slightly flattered by his persistence—and perhaps she was readier than she'd known to yield to his persuasions. She warmed to him because he was so different to Eliot. All the things that Eliot had never been and never could be, she thought. A generous, gentle and considerate man who cared about people and put their needs and well-being before his own, both as a doctor and as a man, she decided.

'Can a girl change her mind about an invitation?' she asked on a sudden impulse, covering the strong, surgeon's hand that lay on the bar counter with her own. 'You said something about a show. Is the offer still open, by any chance?'

'It is—and it's a woman's prerogative to change her mind,' he reminded her lightly, glad that he hadn't got around to inviting someone else and hoping that her sudden and unexpected change of heart heralded a warmer and more satisfying relationship between them.

Hard-working doctors needed to relax with a pretty girl at the end of a long day on a ward, or in theatre, or rushed off their feet in A and E, or battling with the long queues of sick and sometimes disgruntled people in out-patients, and they couldn't afford the kind of affair that might lead to marriage. So they tended to date a variety of nurses they met in the course of their work and often acquired a reputation for flirtation as a result. Nurses understood the demands of the job and made allowances for last-minute cancellation of dates or urgent calls back to the ward or theatre. But there hadn't been as many girls in Trevor's life as the grapevine declared and the wide-eyed juniors loved to imagine— and there'd never been anyone quite like Claudia.

He'd gone on wanting her long after another man might have given up a seemingly pointless pursuit. But that morning, after yet another rebuff, he'd decided to forget her in the arms of the first willing woman to come his way. Now Claudia was unexpectedly smiling on him with a warmth that took him by surprise and filled him with new hope for the future. But he sensed that it would take time for friendship to develop into a more meaningful relationship. She wasn't the type to be swept off her feet and into bed by any man and he thought it very likely that she was still a virgin. She had an air of being unawakened, unaware, slightly shy, that he found irresistible and utterly enchanting.

'The tickets are for tomorrow night, Claudia,' he went on. 'I'll try to change them if that doesn't suit.'

'Tomorrow night will be fine. I'll look forward to it,' she assured him.

He squeezed her slender fingers. 'There's no strings attached,' he said softly, reassuringly. 'Contrary to rumour put about by hopeful first-years, I'm not a raving sex fiend.'

Claudia smiled at him. 'I think I'd reached that conclusion for myself, you know,' she said lightly.

'You're a girl who takes her time to decide whether or not to trust a man, aren't you?' he teased. 'I must have asked you out a dozen times without success.'

Claudia hesitated. Then she said quietly, 'I'm not very good at trusting men, Trevor.'

'That sounds as if you've been unlucky with your men.'

'There's only been one man and he was a disaster.' It was low, reluctant. She was proud and it wasn't easy to admit that she'd made a stupid and disastrous mistake. But if they were to be friends—and possibly even more one day—then she must be frank with him, she knew. This wasn't the time or the place to tell him the truth, of course. At any moment, Eliot would arrive to claim her.

Trevor's heart contracted at the quiet, painful

admission. He put an arm about her shoulders and bent his blond head to kiss her cheek, uncaring of the curious eyes and whispered speculation of the people around them. 'I'm sorry,' he said gently. 'I'll try to make it up to you if you'll let me, Claudia.' Some bastard had hurt her, he thought angrily. So that explained her reluctance to get involved with him or any other man.

There was a slight flurry of movement as someone went out and a couple entered and through the ensuing gap in the crowd, Claudia caught sight of Eliot. She wondered just how long he'd been standing at the other end of the bar, watching her with Trevor, and if he'd seen the kiss bestowed on her by the surgeon. He regarded them through slightly narrowed eyes and a faintly enigmatic smile hovered about the sensual mouth. She felt absurdly uncomfortable.

Had he seen? And did he dislike watching his wife being kissed by another man, for all the years of separation and obvious indifference? Did he suspect that she had found someone else to love despite her denial? And did she only imagine that glint of mocking amusement in his dark eyes for her apparent choice of a man so different to himself in every way—looks and colouring and build and type?

'Oh, there's my date!' she exclaimed. 'Excuse me, won't you, Trevor? I'll see you later, I expect.' It was a hasty and rather clumsy escape but she didn't want to introduce the two men at this stage, feeling that they belonged in totally separate compartments of her life. And how would she introduce a man as her husband to someone who didn't even know that she was a married woman!

'I'm afraid I was late,' Eliot said as she reached his side.

It wasn't an apology and he didn't seem inclined to

offer an explanation. That had never been his way, Claudia remembered. 'It doesn't matter. We won't stay here, if you don't mind. It's too crowded,' she said directly.

'With people who know you?' He smiled as the colour surged into her face. 'All right, my dear. We'll go somewhere else. My car's parked outside. I thought you might want to leave before it became necessary to introduce me to any of your friends.' He took her hand confidently into his own. 'It might embarrass us both. After all, that left hand is ringless for a reason, isn't it?'

'Not for the reason that you obviously imagine,' Claudia said coldly, withdrawing her hand from his possessive clasp and preceding him through the swing-doors of the pub with her head held high. She was uncomfortably aware that too many people had witnessed their meeting and prompt exit. Eliot was the kind of man who attracted attention. His dark good looks and impressive height and the air of distinction made him instantly remarkable and easily remembered.

She wondered wryly how long it would be before the very attractive newcomer to Pat's was known to everyone as 'Sister Hailey's husband'. The similarity of surnames was enough to start people talking and the rest would inevitably follow, for there were bound to be one or two among the staff who would be prompted by the gossip to recall that she'd once married a doctor from Central.

'Who was the blond Adonis? Current boyfriend?' Eliot's hand went to her elbow to guide her through the stream of traffic to his parked car on the opposite side of the road.

Claudia stiffened with resentment. Not so much at his confident touch but at the easy assumption that he had the right to question, *to sneer*, at her choice of friends.

'Just a friend,' she said firmly. 'Trevor Page. He's a senior surgical registrar at Pat's.' He'd find out the facts for himself soon enough if she didn't tell him—and refusing to name her companion would give the impression that he was important to her, she felt.

'Surgeon? Aiming high, aren't you? Does he know that you're married to a mere paediatrician?'

'I scarcely know it myself,' she returned tartly.

Eliot smiled. 'I haven't been around to remind you. But that's about to be remedied,' he announced, settling her in the passenger seat of the brand-new Mercedes.

Claudia's chin tilted in swift defiance of that coolly confident tone. As he slid behind the steering wheel and switched on the ignition, she said coldly, 'It's rather too late to act the husband, Eliot.'

He glanced at her. 'Who said anything about acting? I might be tempted to play it for real. It's an intriguing situation, don't you think?'

'It's an impossible situation and I shall rely on you not to make it any worse!'

'But you never could rely on me, Claudia. Have you forgotten?' It was soft, mocking, deliberately provocative.

She disdained to reply. Turning her head, she watched the impressive frontage of Pat's slide past as the car gained speed. He was infuriating. He was a threat to her peace of mind, her happiness. He was utterly unwelcome in her life after all this time. How could she ever have believed that she'd love him until the end of time? He was the kind of man that she didn't even like!

Yet he was her husband. Once, she'd been passionately in love and desperate to marry him. She'd lived with him for nearly six months. She'd lain in his arms and longed to please him and stifled the disloyal thought that sex was a very unsatisfactory pastime for a woman.

She'd watched him walk out of her life, powerless to stop him, and known that he'd never come back, for all her loving and longing and hoping.

She'd made a new life for herself without him. A life that held little but hard work and lacked the caring and sharing that someone like herself needed for real fulfilment, it was true. But she had proved that she didn't need Eliot, after all. She wished he hadn't come back to unsettle her and to threaten her comfortable existence and her much-loved job. She wondered if she could stay on at Pat's if he was to be there, a perpetual reminder of the past, constant irritation in the present, a shadow on her future with any other man. But at least her eyes had been opened to the realisation that she no longer loved him. She'd merely clung to a sentimental dream of a man who'd never deserved the gift of her love in the first place.

They went to an Italian restaurant and Claudia made a pretence of eating, toying with the food, while he told her a little about Tanzania and his work at the medical mission. She listened and studied him with eyes that seemed to be seeing him for the very first time . . . seeing beyond the enchantment of his dark good looks and slow smile and velvet voice, to the heart that had probably never loved any woman in the whole of his life.

Eliot broke off abruptly, eyes narrowing. 'Penny for your thoughts, Claudia.'

She was startled. 'Sorry . . . !'

'They must be of more interest than anything I have to say. You aren't listening.' He shrugged, smiled. 'Why should you listen? You've no reason to be interested in what I've been doing all these years. You've been getting on with your own life.'

'Isn't that just what you meant me to do?' she countered, challenging him.

'Of course. And I admire you for doing it so well,' he told her lightly. 'But I haven't done too badly myself, you know. Oates has a reputation for insisting on nothing but the best.'

'I don't know if you're a good doctor, Eliot, but you always knew how to get what you wanted,' she said drily. 'And you were always ambitious.' At the expense of everything else, she thought, with a touch of bitterness. For hadn't the demands of his job always come before the needs of his wife? 'I expect you're aiming for a consultancy.'

'Eventually,' he agreed. 'At the moment, I'm specialising in malnutrition in children. Common enough in the Third World, sadly, and found more often than you'd expect in our welfare state. It doesn't have to be due to neglect or poverty or ignorance. There are a number of clinical causes for the body's inability to take nourishment from the foods that we eat.'

'And you like working with children?' Claudia was curious. He'd never evinced the least desire to have any of his own, she remembered.

'Yes, I do. They're uncritical and uncomplaining and too many of them get a raw deal from life—particularly in the part of the world where I've been working, where the people fight to survive in the most appalling conditions. I want to do something, however small, to alleviate some of that suffering. Too many adults are sick through self-abuse—wrong diet, too much alcohol or tobacco, sexual indulgence, careless living. Children get sick through no fault of their own.' He stopped suddenly. 'Now I *am* boring you—with facts that you know perfectly well,' he sighed. 'That's what you get for listening, I'm afraid. It encourages me to talk too much.'

'I'm not bored.' Claudia studied him, thinking there

were depths to him that she'd never suspected. He was still arrogant and critical, expecting too much from everyone. But she felt that he might have learned some tolerance and compassion and how to give more of himself to relationships. It was much too late for *their* relationship to benefit from any change in him, of course.

He was amused by her scrutiny. 'Thinking that I've changed, Claudia? So have you. We're both very different people these days and we don't know much about each other any more. Getting to know each other all over again should be interesting.'

Claudia disliked the confident assumption that they would meet frequently in the days to come. 'You certainly needed to change. You were extremely selfish and thoughtless and overbearing. The world's worst husband,' she said bluntly.

He smiled, slowly and warmly. 'You never said so at the time. I can't remember that you ever complained or listed my many faults or threw the dishes at me—as I no doubt deserved.'

In truth, she'd been too patient and too generous with her love and loyalty. Living on a pedestal had been damnably uncomfortable and he'd eventually been forced to prove that he was a very ordinary man and not the god that her devotion wanted to make of him. Eventually, he'd been forced to escape.

'Oh, I was a very long-suffering wife,' she agreed, thinking that she'd been an awful fool where he was concerned. She wouldn't make the same mistakes if she married for a second time, she determined—and she'd choose a very different kind of man!

Her thoughts were reflected in the beautiful amber eyes that were her most striking feature, clear and candid and wide-spaced, fringed by gold-tipped long lashes. They studied him in coolly critical assessment, eyes that he hadn't always been able to meet so easily in the days when he'd deceived and disappointed her, knowing that they'd shine with unchanged love when they ought to burn with anger and contempt and reproach. He looked into them with a flicker of regret for the might-have-been and a stirring of the desire that she'd always evoked so swiftly in him. But he had always failed to find the response that he needed in her compliant but chilling embrace.

He wondered if another man had managed to melt the ice and kindle the fire that he'd always felt to be dormant but which he hadn't been able to spark into life. The ice that he just hadn't known how to thaw had been the biggest obstacle to their happiness, driving him into the arms of other women and eventually to leaving her altogether. He'd had little patience and not much understanding in those days. Now, older and wiser, he wanted her still.

He slid his hand across the table to capture her slender fingers in a strong, warm clasp. 'You were a very good wife in some ways.'

Claudia raised a sceptical eyebrow. 'That's why you left me?' she said, coolly ironic. She drew her hand from his clasp, unmoved by his touch, the glow in his dark eyes or the smile that warmed his sensual mouth.

It was all so unreal. In a moment, she would probably wake up in her bed and discover that it had all been a strange and rather disturbing, but easily forgotten dream. For it was just too unlikely that Eliot, of all men, should be reaching for her hand and smiling into her eyes as if he wished that they could turn back the years and begin again.

'Unfortunately, you came along too soon,' Eliot told her lightly.

'What does that mean?' Claudia demanded.

'It means that I met you long before I was ready for marriage and its demands. It means that I simply couldn't handle the responsibility for your happiness while I was still so concerned with my own. It wasn't a personal thing, Claudia. It would have turned out the same, no matter which woman I'd married at that particular time. Selfish and thoughtless just about sums up the man that you married,' he confessed.

'You did have some good points,' she said quickly, trying to be fair.

He smiled that slow, mocking smile. 'Don't try to list them. The sky won't fall if you confess to loving me less than you thought you did—or not at all, come to that! It doesn't matter a two-penny damn to me, my dear. I'm not sentimental about a disastrous marriage and I don't see any reason for you to be, either. I'm just sorry that it ever happened.'

She wondered why those brutally blunt words didn't hurt. Surely they ought to hurt? If only because she'd once loved him so much and married him with such high hopes—and suffered as all her illusions about him were shattered, one by one.

'So am I,' she said, with feeling.

'I'm glad to hear it.' Eliot leaned back in his chair, smiling. 'Admitting that we both made a mistake is the first step towards doing something to put matters right.'

'And there's obviously only one way to do that,' Claudia declared swiftly, firmly.

His smile deepened with a hint of mocking amusement. 'Oh, I'm not asking you to forgive and forget, my dear. I'm not suggesting that we try again. I'm not cut out to spend my life with one woman, I'm afraid. I just want to clear the air so that we share the blame, Claudia. I suspect that I've been the villain of the piece all these years. The dirty dog who ruined your life and broke your heart.'

She flushed slightly. 'Not exactly. I know I made mistakes. We asked too much of each other, Eliot. We were too young and full of misplaced confidence and absurd dreams. Next time, we'll both know better and expect less from our partners—and I'm sure that you'll eventually meet someone who you will want to be with for the rest of your life,' she added lightly. 'So I think we should do something about a divorce, don't you? There's really no point in clinging to the past any longer.'

At last she was ready to admit that she wished to be free of the past, free to enjoy the present, free to make plans for a very different future . . . with someone else.

At last she was ready to accept that not only the marriage but the love that had swept her into it and kept her captive all these years was finally at an end.

Admission and acceptance had been a long time coming but she had obviously needed this unexpected encounter with Eliot to clarify the way she felt and just what she wanted.

She no longer loved him at all. She didn't want to stay married to him.

Her heart was her own again and relieved of the burden of unwanted and unrequited love that it had carried for much too long.

CHAPTER FOUR

RETURNING to the ward later that afternoon, Claudia was met by a minor crisis that promptly pushed Eliot and everything else out of her mind for the time being.

Stepping out of the lift, she saw one of her elderly patients weaving drunkenly from side to side in the corridor. Bare-footed, wearing only an unreliable pair of pyjama trousers, he wandered down the deserted corridor with glazed eyes, muttering incoherently to himself. The sound of cheerful voices came from the sluice and the rattle of crockery and cutlery from the ward kitchen. It was that quiet period of the afternoon when patients were entertaining their visitors in the ward or the day-room and the ward staff were able to relax some of their vigilance.

But not all of it, Claudia thought grimly, wondering how Mr Stevens had managed to pull out a nasal tube, detach a drip from his arm and get out of bed without being stopped by a nurse or another patient. He'd had a coleostomy operation only a few days before and was in no condition to be wandering about aimlessly. What on earth had happened to her well-run ward in her brief absence?

'Come along, Mr Stevens,' she said firmly, taking him by the arm and leading him back to the ward. 'You should be in bed.'

'Got to feed me pigeons, gel . . .' His voice was heavy, slurred. He was confused and bewildered, disorientated by drugs. 'Ain't fed 'em for days. Poor little bleeders must be starving . . .'

'They're fine, Mr Stevens. Your son has been going along to feed them every day for you. Don't you remember?'

'My boy Terry? That's a good boy, that is. Good to his old Dad.' He looked about him, puzzled, trembling. 'What's this place, then, gel? Where'd they put me pigeons?'

A first-year hurtled through the ward doors just fractionally before Claudia and the confused old man reached them, obviously in pursuit of the missing patient. She stopped short, her pretty face a study in mingled relief, dismay and apprehension.

Observing the cap perched uncertainly on thick fair curls, the crumpled apron and the stricken face, Claudia wasn't at all surprised to find that Carol Gray was responsible for yet another near-disaster. She was very disappointed. Having taken the girl severely to task only that morning and warned her that she was on the verge of being on Matron's report, she'd expected better things.

'Oh, Sister! Mr Stevens! I only turned my back for a moment!' She broke off, knowing that was no excuse for her failure to keep a constant vigil on a patient who'd already tried three times to pull out the tube that he disliked so much.

'That's all it needs, Nurse,' Claudia said tartly.

'Yes, Sister. I'm sorry, Sister.'

'Take Mr Stevens into the ward, put him back to bed and make him comfortable, Nurse. Ask Nurse Murray to keep a careful eye on him and then report to me.'

'Yes, Sister.' It wasn't Claudia Hailey's policy to scold anyone in front of a patient or within sight or sound of another member of staff and the juniors liked and respected her for that. But she was very strict when it came to anything that seemed to smack of neglect of her patients and the gleam in the amber eyes warned Carol Gray that the reprimand was only postponed. She stifled a sigh. She'd been making a real effort to please in the last few days but she was still living up to her reputation as a walking disaster area, she thought unhappily. Now Sister would be convinced that she was lazy and irresponsible and incapable of making the grade as a nurse. She might even send her to Matron. Blow Mr Stevens and his pigeons!

'I shall be in my office, paging Mr Craven,' Claudia said pointedly. 'He'll need to make a special visit to replace that tube and set up another drip. I'm afraid you won't be very popular, Nurse Gray.'

'No, Sister . . .' The chastened first-year put an arm about Mr Stevens and began to coax him back into the ward.

Claudia turned away. She could do both jobs herself, of course. But the young houseman would be irritated by the extra work and would no doubt utter a few scathing remarks on the general incompetence of junior nurses. And that would probably have more of an impact on the girl, who had a soft spot for him, than anything she could say to her, Claudia thought dryly, remembering her own first-year days.

She went along to her office and found her staff nurses relaxing over a tray of tea. They were hard-working and conscientious nurses whom she'd known and worked with for some time and she knew they had earned their brief respite from ward chores. Smiling, she shook her head to Lesley Wilmot's instant offer of tea.

'No, thanks.' Whisking her cloak from her shoulders, she stored it in a cupboard. 'I've just prevented Mr Stevens from running home to his blessed pigeons,' she said, carefully light. 'Can anyone tell me why the ward seems to be in the sole charge of a scatter-brained first year?' It wasn't quite a reproach but her tone queried the wisdom of both staff nurses being absent from the ward at the same time.

'It isn't. Soames is about somewhere,' Lesley said serenely, referring to the third-year she'd delegated to take responsibility for the ward while she thankfully put her feet up for ten minutes.

'Probably flirting with the footballer in bed three behind drawn curtains,' Julie Gordon said shrewdly, getting reluctantly to her feet and moving towards the door. 'I'll go and rout her out. Did the old fellow actually make it out of bed this time, Sister?'

'He did, indeed. I found him in the corridor minus tube, minus drip and almost minus trousers,' Claudia said coolly.

'Oh, God! Where is he now?'

'He might have been halfway down the High Street,' she pointed out, 'but he's being put back to bed by Nurse Gray.'

'I'll go and give her a hand. She'll never manage him,' Julie said with the resignation of experience. 'He's very stubborn and a bit cantankerous and he doesn't take much notice of the juniors. Bits of girls, he calls them. He calls me missus and makes me feel about forty!' She went out, tugging at her apron.

'He seemed to go right off to sleep after his injection,' Lesley said carefully. 'I thought he'd be all right without an armed guard and told Carol Gray that she needn't 'special' as long as she checked him regularly.' She sighed. 'So I'm really to blame and I hope you won't wipe the floor with the poor child.'

Claudia sat down at her desk. 'I'm glad you confessed before I sent her to Matron!'

Lesley smiled. 'You're rather hard on her, aren't you?' She wondered if her senior had a personal grudge against the pretty and flirtatious junior. Perhaps she'd noticed the way that Trevor Page's blue eyes rested on the girl at times—and it was no secret to her nurses that the reserved and reticent Sister Hailey had a soft spot for the surgeon.

Claudia looked her surprise. 'Am I? No more than the other juniors, surely?' She thought about it for a moment or two. Then she nodded. 'You may be right,' she conceded fairly. 'The thing is that she's a bright girl, with all the potential and promise of a really good nurse—and it annoys me that she's so haphazard on the ward. She's an incorrigible flirt, too. I suppose I do get impatient, but I wouldn't want her to feel that I've a particular down on her. I must try to be more tolerant.' She reached for the telephone. 'Now, I must get hold of George Craven. The drip is still essential but I'm hoping that he'll decide against replacing the stomach tube. The poor old man hates it so and it would probably be coming out tomorrow, in any case.'

'I'd better get on. It's almost time for the drugs round.' Lesley wandered off with the deceptively dreamy air that typified her and Claudia set about contacting the houseman. At last he answered his bleeper by heading for the nearest telephone, and when she'd explained the situation he promised to come up to the ward right away.

In view of Lesley's explanation and a slight pricking of her conscience where the junior was concerned, there was little that Claudia could say to the repentant Carol Gray. But she did extract one more promise of greater effort in her practical work.

Absorbed in her own work, Claudia had little time to think about that unexpected lunch with Eliot until the end of the day when she was walking the short distance to the tall block of modern apartments in a turning off the High Street, where she shared a flat with another nurse. Leonie had been her closest friend since early training days and she was possibly the only person left at Pat's who would remember Eliot and knew all about that unhappy marriage and its inevitable outcome. Claudia had always felt that her secrets were safe with her friend. Now, she wondered how Leonie would react to the news that Eliot was coming to work at Pat's. She'd never liked or trusted him. Her instincts about men had always been much better developed and far more reliable than my own, Claudia thought wryly.

Currently working as a staff nurse on Matthew, one of the children's wards, Leonie was likely to see much more of a medical registrar on a paediatric firm than herself, of course. It would be surprising if Eliot, always an opportunist, didn't make some kind of overture to her pretty friend. But he was sure to be snubbed, Claudia thought confidently.

Leonie was small and slight with a cluster of blonde curls and expressive grey eyes, delicately pretty and appealingly feminine. Her deceptive air of fragility made everyone wonder if she had the strength and the stamina for nursing. She'd been off duty for a couple of days and the flat was sparkling like a new pin when Claudia walked in. They took it in turns to clean and cook and launder, week by week, and it was a system that worked well. Leonie was a good and imaginative cook and she enjoyed housework—and she was marvellous with children. Claudia believed that she'd make some man a wonderful wife one day—but heaven knew when! For while there were plenty of men in her friend's life, she seemed to be genuinely uninterested in marriage—and that was an attitude that was much appreciated by hard-up young doctors and medical students!

Claudia tossed cloak and bag on to the sofa and turned

down the radio that was playing rather too loudly. 'Hi! I'm home!' she called.

'In the bedroom.' It was a vague reply. Leonie was obviously getting ready for yet another date. There were few evenings that she didn't spend with one or other of her men-friends.

Claudia paused on the threshold of the room and watched Leonie carefully applying her make-up. 'I saw Eliot today,' she announced, non-committally. 'He took me to lunch.'

'That was nice . . .' Leonie was intent on applying just the right amount of blusher. Then the words registered and she swung abruptly to look intently at Claudia. '*What* did you say?'

She obligingly repeated it. 'I had lunch with Eliot.'

Leonie searched her face, wondering, eyes narrowed. 'Eliot Hailey, do you mean? Your Eliot?'

Claudia smiled at the inapt choice of words. 'The one and only.'

'How, why and where?' Leonie demanded, agog. 'And why didn't you tell me that you were meeting him? How could you keep it to yourself?'

'I didn't know a thing until it happened. He came to Pat's for a job interview, then came up to the ward in search of me and suggested we have some lunch together.'

'Just like that!'

Claudia nodded. 'Just like that. He strolled into the ward as if he'd never been away. Typically Eliot.' She smiled at the memory.

'It would be! And I suppose you were absolutely delighted to see him—and it showed!' Leonie shook her head at her friend in resigned reproach. 'Will you never learn? After what he did to you, I don't know how you could even speak to him, let alone welcome him with open arms—but I bet that's just what you did! In your shoes, I'd have been living with another man by this time. You're so strong,' she said, wonderingly. 'So loyal!'

'So stupid?' Claudia suggested.

'That, too,' Leonie told her bluntly. 'He was never worth it.'

Claudia didn't wince. It wasn't meant to hurt. Leonie was only concerned for the wasted years and the heartache. She'd never understood that the love of nursing and the satisfaction she'd found in her job all these years had compensated for the lack of husband, home and children. Time and again, she'd forgotten the ache in her heart and the lingering emptiness in her life as she busied herself about the ward and dealt with much greater problems than lost love, a broken marriage. There'd never been the time or the inclination for too much self-pity.

'It was nice to know that he's well—and doing well,' she said lightly. 'He's just come back from Tanzania.'

'That's a pity. I suppose he's as full of himself as ever.' Leonie had never liked him. Not even for Claudia could she pretend to be pleased that he'd turned up like the proverbial bad penny.

'I wouldn't say so. I thought he'd changed in many ways.' Claudia sat down on the edge of Leonie's bed and kicked off the flat-heeled brogues that were so essential to a nurse's day but so unflattering to a girl's legs. 'Oh, I know you think I'm mad but I was really pleased to see him after the initial shock. You can't imagine how often I've wondered about him and wished that he'd get in touch, if only to let me know that he's well and happy.'

'Oh, I can,' Leonie murmured, caustically. She looked at her friend with slight anxiety. 'I hope you aren't about to do anything silly. Like going back to him and letting him make you miserable all over again!'

Claudia shook her head. 'He doesn't want me back.' She said it without the smallest twinge of pain or regret, further proof that she was really over him at last.

'He told you so, no doubt. That sounds just like the Eliot we know and love,' Leonie said.

'He didn't have to say it. It's much too late for us to start again. We've both changed, become very different people.' She was unconsciously quoting Eliot as she spoke. 'We're almost strangers after so long.'

Leonie wasn't impressed by the cool, matter of fact tone. She knew that Claudia had never stopped loving or hoping all these years. She was that kind of girl, she thought, torn between admiration for such single-minded love and devotion and impatience that Claudia had wasted it all on a man who just wasn't worth it.

'Oh, you'd be over the moon if he did want you back,' she declared with the forgivable frankness of long and close friendship. 'But it would end in just the same way and you know it, Claudia. He'd use you while it suited him and walk out when he got bored or found someone else.' She frowned suddenly. 'Did you say that he's after a job at Pat's?'

'He's got it. A very good job, too.' Claudia crossed one slender leg over the other and studied a run in her sheer black stocking in slight dismay. 'Registrar to Sir Hartley . . .'

Leonie bridled instantly. 'You mean they're letting him loose among my babies!' The infants on Matthew were very dear to her heart and she'd been known to stand up to Sir Hartley himself when she hadn't agreed with a treatment that he'd prescribed for one of them.

Claudia couldn't help smiling at the indignation in her friend's eyes and voice. 'He isn't a monster! He must be a very good doctor if Sir Hartley's taken him on his firm. Be fair!'

'He probably charmed his way into the job. He was always good at that kind of thing.' She turned back to the mirror, picking up a lipstick. 'So he took you to lunch? That was generous.'

Claudia ignored the sarcasm. 'It was rather too rushed for all we had to talk about, of course.'

'Is it too much to hope that you found time to talk about getting a divorce?' It was blunt, practical, like Leonie herself. She finished outlining her lips and looked directly into Claudia's eyes, reflected in the mirror, challenging.

Claudia hesitated. 'You know that I could have divorced him long ago. You know that I never wanted to do it. I had my reasons.'

'I know.' Impulsively, Leonie moved from the stool to the bed beside her friend and put an arm about her shoulders. Claudia wasn't saying much because that wasn't her way. She'd never been a whiner but she was obviously upset and unsettled by the unexpected encounter with her swine of a husband. 'You cherished a lovely dream that he'd realise all he'd thrown away and come back to you one day,' she said gently. 'Well, it hasn't happened and I think you finally knew today that it never will. I'm sorry, love. I do know how you feel about him, but you've wasted so many years. Don't waste any more!'

Claudia agreed that it was time to sever the link and put a failed marriage behind her. She'd expected Eliot to be of the same mind and she was surprised that he'd actively resisted her suggestion of an amicable divorce.

He wouldn't make waves if she really wanted her freedom, he'd assured her smoothly. But if she was content with things as they were and had no desire to re-marry at present, where was the urgency? In fact it would suit him to stay married for the time being. He'd admitted that with a disarming frankness. Apparently Sir Hartley preferred his registrars to be married men— and he hadn't felt it necessary to tell him that he was actually separated from his wife, he'd added with a slight smile.

Claudia suspected that it suited him in other ways to have a wife in the background, one who didn't make demands on him or interfere with his freedom but protected him from the hopeful persuasions of women who fell in love with him and would like to marry him. It didn't really matter to her, of course. She was used to being married in name only.

'I know you never liked him,' she said carefully, smiling at Leonie. 'But he isn't all bad, and there's really no reason why we can't be civilised about the situation and be friends.'

'*Friends!*' Leonie almost exploded. 'Oh, well—it's your life,' she conceded abruptly. She supposed that Claudia couldn't help it if she was still so much in love that she snatched at straws. Thank heavens that she'd never felt that intensely about any man—and probably never would. She'd hate to swallow all her pride and self-respect just because she'd fallen in love!

'We're bound to run into each other occasionally now that he'll be working at Pat's. It isn't an easy situation but we don't have to make it worse for each other, Leonie. He's been out of the country for three years and lost touch with people and places and it would be unkind of me to refuse to meet him sometimes, to be friendly. He has to get used to a new job—and he needs to find somewhere convenient to live, too. I said I'd look at flats with him. No harm in that, is there? I'd do as much for a stranger.'

It was defensive, forestalling the militant sparkle in her friend's grey eyes and the words that were obviously hovering on Leonie's lips. 'I daresay I'm a fool but I can't hate him. It isn't his fault that he stopped loving me and it may even have been mine, after all.'

Leonie stared. 'You sound almost sorry for him!'

Claudia smiled, shook her head. 'No, not that. I can't imagine feeling sorry for Eliot. He's much too self-assured, too self-sufficient. He really doesn't need me— or anyone else.'

'Then leave him to find a flat by himself—and find his feet in the new job without your help!'

'I expect it would be more sensible,' Claudia agreed levelly. 'And I certainly don't owe him anything. But I'm still his wife.' She shrugged. 'He isn't asking so very much of me, I suppose.'

She'd been astonished that he'd asked anything at all. It seemed so out of character for a man like Eliot to admit that he'd appreciate her help in finding a flat in the near neighbourhood and that he'd like to meet her from time to time while he was settling down after all the years out of England. He'd suggested with a very disarming smile that there was no reason why they couldn't be friends, even if they'd found it impossible to live together—and Claudia had felt that it would be churlish to reject the extended olive branch.

She knew that she didn't love him any more but perhaps she wasn't entirely immune to the lingering charm of his smile and the glow in his dark eyes or the warm persuasion of the deep, velvet voice. And maybe she found it rather flattering that he seemed to be impressed by the woman she'd become in his absence. She knew she'd matured, acquired a new and becoming confidence—and she would need to be blind or stupid not to know that she was attractive to men.

It wouldn't be so surprising if Eliot desired her all over again, she felt. He'd always been a sensual man and perhaps he'd forgotten the frigidity that had marred their marriage—or thought she'd overcome it. He couldn't know that there hadn't been another man in her life since he'd left her. That was due as much to the deep-rooted anxiety that she would disappoint yet another man with her lack of response to lovemaking as to her conviction that she could never love anyone but Eliot and didn't want to replace him with someone else.

She couldn't help her frigidity. It seemed that she was simply one of those women who were destined never to respond to a man's touch, a man's embrace, in the way that he wanted and expected. Her lack of response had struck at Eliot's male pride, she knew. A man liked to feel that a woman melted before the heat of his passion and was powerless to resist his sexuality and her own desire. She'd tried to pretend but she'd been too inexperienced to be convincing and she knew that she'd disappointed him again and again.

In such circumstances, their marriage hadn't really had much of a chance of surviving, she admitted with a new understanding. No wonder she was beginning to feel that Eliot might be forgiven for deserting her for another woman. No wonder she was beginning to accept that she had failed him just as much as he'd failed her. No wonder she was prepared to take him back as a friend if not as a husband . . .

CHAPTER FIVE

HAVING found the record she wanted, Claudia took it from its colourful sleeve and placed it on the stereo turntable. Then, as the music flowed into the room, she went back to her chair with a smile for Trevor that didn't betray her slight nervousness.

She relaxed in her chair, very slender and lovelier than she knew in the ivory silk suit that she'd worn for the theatre, gleaming hair swept into a knot of curls high on her head. Trevor stretched his long legs and eased himself more comfortably on the sofa cushions, sipping his drink, studying her through slightly narrowed eyes.

It wasn't that she didn't trust him, Claudia assured herself firmly. It was simply that the quickened beat of her heart didn't necessarily mean that her senses would also quicken to the kind of response that he would expect when he eventually reached to take her into his arms. For, like any man, he must have construed her impulsive suggestion of a nightcap as an invitation to lovemaking, she thought a little cynically.

She wondered what had prompted her to invite the good-looking blond surgeon into the flat at this late hour after months of keeping him at a careful distance. It was just the kind of encouragement that he'd hoped for and she'd meant to avoid, reluctant to raise his hopes and afraid of disappointing him. For her heart and mind were capable of yearning but her body stayed cold, unawakened and unwilling.

Loving Eliot, married to him, she'd given her body gladly even while she marvelled that he found so much pleasure and satisfaction in the sexual encounter. There was no way that she could ever welcome another man as a lover if both love and desire on her part were lacking, she determined.

She wasn't naive. She knew that Trevor would expect to take her to bed if she continued to go out with him on a regular basis. He made no secret of wanting her and sex seemed to be an essential part of any relationship in this permissive day and age.

She liked Trevor. She felt that he had all the qualities that she most admired and respected in a man. But she didn't want to get too involved at this stage. Having regained her heart after so long, she didn't want to let it out of her keeping again too soon. And he was the kind of man that she might find easy to love if she allowed it to happen.

She'd enjoyed the evening, the trip to the theatre, the meal after the show. She'd warmed to him, conscious that he liked her more than a little, convinced that this first date might be the prelude to many—if she wished. But there was a secret that she must share with him if she wanted to go on dating him.

She drew a deep breath. Trevor looked at her with a gleam of enquiry in his blue eyes—and her courage failed her abruptly. 'This is the number I particularly liked in the show,' she said instead, as music filled the room, sweet and throbbing, reviving memories of the darkened theatre and the colourful extravaganza, linked hands and exchanged smiles and glances of appreciation, the rapport of liking and friendship.

Trevor nodded, remembering. 'It was a great evening, Claudia. Perhaps we could do it again some time.' It was hopeful, probing.

She was still keeping him at a distance, he thought ruefully. It was only to be expected on the ward where etiquette had to be observed and there were too many eyes and ears to take note of any personal exchange between registrar and sister. But having finally persuaded her to go out with him, he'd hoped for a degree of encouragement that he just wasn't getting.

He'd brought her home and she'd invited him in for a drink, put on some music and chatted lightly and politely about the evening in a cool, friendly fashion that kept him effectively at bay. Now, she was regarding him with an expression in the beautiful amber eyes that he couldn't quite fathom. But he didn't think it was encouragement!

It had been a pleasant evening without being memorable. Claudia had been delightful but distant, friendly but formal. It seemed to Trevor that he'd said and done all the right things with very little result and it was frustrating.

He wanted her very much—and it was more than the physical desire that he'd felt for women in the past. For him, it was the beginning of love and it rested with Claudia whether he crushed it before it took possession of him, body and soul, or allowed it full rein.

She hesitated. 'Maybe . . . I don't know—perhaps.' For once, her usual cool confidence deserted her as she met his warm gaze with its hint of affection and a great deal of promise.

He still smiled but it was tinged with a touch of dismay. 'Meaning no? Going to tell me that Matron wouldn't approve?'

'Matron doesn't have to know,' she said slowly. 'But it's perfectly true that she wouldn't approve. In the circumstances.' It was time to tell him what the circumstances actually were, she knew.

He raised an eyebrow, amused. 'Sisters have been known to date doctors and Pat's hasn't crumbled from the shock.' He studied her thoughtfully. 'Trying to let me down lightly, Claudia?'

'I don't want to let you down at all,' she said impulsively. 'Tonight has been fun and I've really enjoyed it. I'd forgotten how good it feels to spend an evening with an attentive and very attractive man.' She smiled at him warmly, gratefully.

Trevor wondered at the candour that betrayed an astonishing lack of men in this lovely girl's life. How little he knew about her for all the months of knowing her. She had a gift for inspiring trust and the genuine warmth of her interest and concern for others encouraged patients and junior nurses to confide in her, sure of a sympathetic hearing. But if Claudia had problems, she apparently kept them to herself, solved them for herself. He felt that she was more vulnerable than she would admit and he was moved to a tender longing to take care of the girl who behaved as though she didn't need anyone to look after her. The coolly efficient ward sister was a woman like any other, away from the aseptic and inhibiting atmosphere of the hospital.

'I'm rather puzzled,' he said quietly. 'You're such a lovely girl. I can't believe that there haven't been lots of men after you, lots of invitations. You must have a reason for turning them all down.'

'I have.' It was quick and crisp and defensive. Claudia rose to take the now-silent record from the stereo turntable, finding it harder than she'd expected to explain to someone as concerned and as kind and as nice as Trevor that she'd made a very stupid mistake and mortgaged her happiness by marrying the wrong man. She valued his good opinion more than she'd known, she thought ruefully.

As she passed him, Trevor shot out a hand to capture her slender wrist. She looked down at him, startled, slightly wary. 'I'm not going to pry,' he said gently. 'You don't have to tell me anything. But I suspect that I'm having to pay the penalty for another man's fault. You might give me a chance to prove that we aren't all tarred with the same brush.'

His smile was so warm, his touch so reassuring and his words so unexpectedly perceptive that Claudia felt a rush of affection for him. For much too long she'd been proudly insisting that she didn't need a man in her life, that men were incapable of real and lasting emotions and that Trevor would only hurt and abandon her if she was fool enough to relent and give in to his persuasions. But all the pride, all the bitterness, all the distrust didn't make her feel less like a woman when he smiled and took her hand to his lips to press a kiss into the palm.

He seemed to offer the kind of reassurance that a woman needed when she'd been badly hurt and bitterly humiliated and had taken much too long to get over it. There might even be a few moments of magic to be found in his arms, and she was desperately in need of a little magic in her life.

On a sudden impulse, she bent to kiss him—and then his arms were about her and he was drawing her down to the sofa, eager and encouraged by a gesture that she'd instantly regretted. But she found that going into his arms was the easiest thing in the world, after all. For they closed about her with a kind of tenderness rather than passion and his lips were warm and gentle against her own, giving rather than demanding, so that she was persuaded to relax and allow his kiss to linger and deepen.

His embrace was pleasant and reassuring but it failed to excite her to the flood of desire that might coax her to forget everything. His hands moved over her shoulders and her slender back in a sensuous caress and his kiss gradually became more persuasive, more ardent. She felt him draw down the long zip of her frock, and then he was touching her, caressing her, with sure but gentle hands. An instinctive murmur of protest was stifled by the hardening hunger of his mouth. He drew the thin silk from her shoulders and the firm, tilting breasts and raised his head to look at her and she heard the soft catch of his breath in mingled admiration and desire.

He turned her in his arms and bent his blond head to kiss her bare breasts, and Claudia allowed him to make light and potentially dangerous love to her. She liked him so much and wished with all her heart that she liked his kiss, his caress, the ardent pressure of his urgent body against her own, as she should. As any normal woman probably would, she thought, near to despair. She could sense the rising passion in him, nearing fever pitch, and she tried to draw away, to check the strong hands in their sensual exploration.

'Oh, Claudia,' he said softly, ardent, voice husky with longing. 'Don't refuse me when I want you so much . . . when I've wanted you for so long. Let me make love to you—please, darling.' He kissed her again, tried to draw her closer.

How difficult it was for a woman to say no and mean it, even when she wasn't even tempted to say yes! Claudia breathed a sigh of regret for his disappointment—and her own. For, deep down, she'd almost convinced herself that he was the one man who could release the surging spring of desire in the secret places of her body and teach her the meaning of a kind of loving that seemed to bring heaven within the reach of everyone but herself. Sadly, it just hadn't happened.

'I can't. I'm sorry—I can't,' she said, almost desperately, resisting him, slender hands clenched fiercely against his chest to keep him at bay. 'Not now—not yet.'

'Not ever, I expect,' Trevor said quietly, dismayed and despairing. He released her abruptly and straightened, struggling to master the surging tide of passion, thrusting his hands through the thick thatch of blond hair.

'I don't know . . .' She saw the unsteady throb of the pulse in his cheek and the disappointment in the blue eyes. She put a tentative hand on his shoulder. 'I'm sorry, Trevor, truly I am.'

She hadn't meant things to go so far. She'd only kissed him on an impulse. Then she'd welcomed the comfort of his arms about her and the soothing balm of his kiss for a heart that could still ache for another man's indifference and desertion. But she couldn't explain. She couldn't make that kind of bid for his sympathy. She was much too proud.

Trevor rose to his feet in a way that shook off both her touch and her apology. 'I'm not sure that you are,' he said brusquely, hurt and frustration expressing themselves as anger. 'Too many women promise a great deal and give nothing, and assume that saying sorry earns them instant forgiveness. I thought you were different.'

Claudia smarted at the words that lumped her so readily with other women and didn't give her credit for any finer feelings. Did he really think she was capable of a kind of sexual teasing that she had always despised?

'And too many men assume that a kiss or two leads directly to the bedroom,' she retorted defensively, struggling with the elusive zip of her frock.

Trevor turned her with carefully impersonal hands on her shoulders and drew up the long back zip. 'I suppose it would be impossible to convince you that I didn't have sex in mind when I asked you out. I'm up against my reputation and your lack of trust, and it seems to be a combination I can't fight.'

Claudia's heart sank slightly. He was on the point of walking from the flat and out of her life, she realised. She liked him so much and she was more desperate than she'd known for someone to fill the aching void in her life that Eliot had left. She wished she could explain that she wanted to open her arms and maybe even her heart to him but was too afraid of being hurt and let down all over again. She'd never confided in him and now she regretted it.

The front door of the flat was suddenly slammed shut with a careless disregard for the lateness of the hour or sleeping neighbours. Trevor stiffened and shot an enquiring and slightly suspicious glance at Claudia.

Before she could say a word, Leonie burst upon them in all her radiant glory, her hair a cloud about her delicately lovely face.

'Oops!' she exclaimed, grey eyes sparkling with sudden interest as she looked from fair surgeon to a slightly disconcerted Claudia and back again. 'Do I intrude? I hope I haven't shattered a tender moment!' She bestowed her golden smile on them both without favour.

'Only the front door frame and a few ear-drums,' Claudia returned dryly, knowing that Leonie must be all curiosity and amazement, for this was the first time that she'd brought a man to the flat in all the years that they'd shared it.

'Sorry about that,' she laughed, unrepentant. She whisked the gossamer-thin wrap from her shoulders to reveal a clinging, flame-coloured frock that flattered her shapely figure and enhanced her blonde beauty.

'I'm not sure if you already know each other. Trevor Page—Leonie Winters . . .' Claudia was compelled to make the introduction by the way that they looked at each other. She tried not to mind the obvious glint of male admiration in Trevor's eyes or the immediate response in Leonie's smile. 'Trevor was just leaving,' she added lightly.

'Really? Don't rush away on my account. I'm off to bed in a moment.' Leonie smiled at Trevor. 'You're Professor Harding's registrar, aren't you? I've seen you around.' She'd heard about him, too. She was surprised and very curious to find him at the flat in Claudia's company. But, knowing Claudia's attitude to men and her reason for it, she knew that it couldn't be anything but a platonic relationship. So she needn't feel guilty about her own immediate interest in a very good-looking man whom she'd never had the opportunity to meet on a personal basis until now.

Trevor had seen her around, too. She wasn't the type that a man could easily overlook. But she was such a honeypot that he hadn't even tried to fight his way through the crowd of male admirers to bring himself to her notice. She was very lovely, very feminine—and a flirt. He was smarting from Claudia's rebuff but he hadn't yet given up all hope. So the warm interest in Leonie's smiling eyes was merely something to file away for the future if he should need the comfort and consolation of another woman's arms, he decided.

'I used to see you in out-patients, surely?' he countered lightly. 'But that was some time ago. Last year, I should think. We've never been formally introduced but we have been in each other's company on occasions. Various parties. So we do know each other, more or less.'

'Why not make it more?' she suggested promptly. 'I'm working on Matthew these days. Come up and see my babies some time!' It was blatant invitation and encouragement, but only because she was very sure that she wasn't poaching on Claudia's preserves. She would never steal a man from her friend under any circumstances. But Claudia's heart was so firmly set on the man she'd married that Leonie knew that her interest in someone like Trevor Page could only be friendly and casual.

Trevor smiled but didn't commit himself to anything remotely resembling a promise. A few moments later, he declared that he had to be on his way and Claudia went with him to the door, convinced that their first date was destined to be the last, torn between relief and regret that she wasn't likely to be drawn into a relationship that would make demands upon her that she could not meet satisfactorily.

'I'm not sorry that we were so rudely interrupted,' she said, carefully light, smiling at him. 'We were on the verge of quarrelling and I didn't want that to happen.'

He touched her cheek with gentle fingers. 'I was rather sharp with you, I'm afraid. But I certainly had no intention of quarrelling with you!'

'I'm glad,' she said simply.

'No hard feelings?'

'Of course not!'

His kiss was the merest brush of his lips across her own, light and friendly. Then he straightened, smiled. 'We'll play it just the way you want it, Claudia. Just good friends.'

For the time being, he added silently. Until he could persuade her that he was to be trusted not to hurt her as the mystery man that she wasn't talking about had done.

It was goodbye and she knew it, Claudia thought ruefully. Off with the old and on with the new—and, because he was that kind of man, a tactful pause between the two, no doubt. Perhaps it was just as well . . .

Hearing the click of the front door, Leonie came out of her bedroom in a wisp of coffee lace and chiffon, hairbrush in hand. 'I'm sorry,' she said contritely. 'I didn't mean to cramp your style!'

Claudia laughed. 'You didn't. We went to the theatre and had a meal and I asked him in for a drink when he brought me home. Nothing more than that.' It was cool, convincingly casual.

Leonie perched on the arm of the sofa while Claudia tidied the room. 'He's nice, isn't he?'

'Good-looking, too,' Claudia said, teasingly.

Leonie brushed a curl about her fingers, a thoughtful look in her eyes. 'A *really* nice man, I mean. Do you know, I can't remember the last time that you had a date.'

'You know very well that I haven't been out with any man for years. But don't make too much of it, Leonie. I like Trevor Page well enough but that's as far as it goes.'

'He likes you a lot!'

'Oh, I don't know. We get on well during working hours and I suppose you could say that we're good friends,' Claudia conceded. 'But it isn't a close relationship, by any means. He's asked me out several times but I've always felt that it wouldn't work away from Pat's—and I was right, as it happens. I'm not really his type and I don't think he'll ask again.' It was coolly matter of fact.

'He made a pass and you didn't like it,' Leonie interpreted shrewdly.

Claudia laughed but a hint of betraying warmth rose in her face. 'Oh, go to bed, you horrid creature!' she exclaimed lightly.

Leonie smiled, triumphant. 'Then I'm right! And I suppose you froze the poor man!'

'You may thaw him out with my blessing.'

'I might, too. Given half a chance,' Leonie said

promptly. 'I've always liked what I've heard about him, I must admit.'

'You're much more his type than I am—and I expect he realises that now. I was a dreadful disappointment to him, I suspect. Why must men always think that I'm playing hard to get when I really don't want to know?' She sighed.

Leonie looked at her curiously. 'Eliot seems to have put you off men for life.'

Claudia shrugged. 'I think it's just the way I'm made,' she said, a little defensively. It was as near as she could ever get to admitting the frigidity that had been the curse of her marriage and might prove to be the death knell of every relationship with a man for the rest of her life.

She didn't feel it was fair to allow Eliot to be blamed for something that wasn't his fault, something that he hadn't suspected or expected when he'd fallen in love with her and asked her to marry him. How naive she'd been, too—supposing that a wedding-ring on her finger would immediately spark the essential response to his lovemaking that had been lacking throughout their brief courtship.

Eliot had accepted her insistence on staying a virgin until they were married with some reluctance. Loving him, she'd been so sure that things would come right once they were married. But they hadn't, and he'd never really forgiven her for deceiving him. He hadn't been a good husband, by any means. But she'd cheated him from the very beginning and no doubt she hadn't deserved anything more than she'd got from that disastrous marriage.

'Oh, that's nonsense!' Leonie declared stoutly, shrewd and worldly-wise enough to suspect the flaw in her friend's make-up that she never actually admitted. 'You just haven't met the right man. But one day you will and then you'll forget all about Eliot and be really happy at last. And I hope that Eliot realises what he threw away and suffers the tortures of the damned when that day dawns! But I don't suppose he will. That man was never capable of loving anyone but himself and I doubt very much if he's changed at all.' She got up from the sofa, stretching. 'Well, I'm off to bed—and if you're quite sure that you don't want Trevor Page then I might allow myself to dream about him,' she added, lightening the moment and the mood with the mischief in her grey eyes.

Claudia smiled. 'Sweet dreams,' she said brightly, refusing to admit to a little pang. But she did like Trevor, very much.

He might have figured prominently in Leonie's dreams that night but he was absent from her own. However, Claudia woke to the thought of him and the decision to tell him at the earliest possible moment that she was not only married but that her husband had returned to the scene after four long years. She owed it to Trevor to be honest, she felt. Indeed, she felt guilty that she hadn't been frank with him from the beginning . . .

CHAPTER SIX

CLAUDIA was off duty that weekend and she'd promised to spend her precious Saturday flat-hunting with Eliot. It seemed uncomfortably poignant to be getting ready to go out with him again after so long and she couldn't help remembering the early days when she'd dressed for their dates with her heart beating faster for the mere thought of being with him.

Now, her heart quickened with a kind of trepidation as she took particular pains with her face and hair, for he had always been critical of the way she looked. He'd liked her to follow fashion, too, and she felt that he would approve of the stylish yellow, cream and tan striped silk suit with its straight jacket and full skirt and ruffled collar, the newest item in her wardrobe. It was a relief to exchange the flat-heeled brogues for the elegance of high-heeled court shoes, too.

She hadn't seen Eliot since they'd had lunch together at the beginning of the week. He'd told her that he was going to Dorset to spend a few days with his family before taking up his appointment at Pat's but would be back in good time to keep their date on Saturday.

She hadn't seen Trevor, either. She'd been at a sisters' conference in Matron's office one morning when he came to do his round and Lesley Wilmot had been in charge of the ward. She'd gone to early lunch another day when he was later than usual in arriving. And she was busy in a side-ward with a very ill patient who she couldn't leave when he came on a third occasion to examine a new admission before surgery.

It was frustrating that she hadn't found an opportunity to talk to him. She wanted to explain about Eliot before he began his new job the following week. She knew that the grapevine would be humming with speculation about the new registrar and she suspected that the revelation of 'Sister Hailey's husband' would be all over the hospital in no time.

She emerged from her bedroom, wondering if Eliot would be punctual that morning. 'How do I look?' she asked, a little anxiously, needing the reassurance.

Leonie looked up from her breakfast toast and her letters and surveyed her with comprehensive approval. 'Very smart!' she declared. 'I do like that suit. *A la* Princess Di—and you've the height and the figure to carry it off, too! Is this all for Eliot's benefit? He doesn't deserve it.'

Claudia wrinkled her nose at her outspoken friend. 'It's for *my* benefit,' she said firmly. 'It's nice to feel like a woman after having to be starchy Sister Hailey all the week!'

Actually, she didn't feel as confident as she could wish. It had been easier to deal with Eliot when she was in uniform and could rely on her role of competent ward sister for moral support. She was feeling rather apprehensive about spending several hours with him in very different clothes and surroundings and circumstances. She wondered what they would find to talk about when their lives had followed such different paths that they'd become virtual strangers. She wondered why he wanted to pick up the threads of their torn and tattered relationship when he obviously had no regrets and no lingering sentiment where she was concerned.

'What time is he supposed to be here?' Leonie remembered his reputation for lateness, too.

'Ten o'clock.' Claudia glanced at the wall clock. It

wanted a few minutes to the hour. She knew he would be late, as always, but nevertheless her lips were suddenly dry and a pulse began to hammer in the hollow of her throat.

'I suppose I should dress.' Leonie drew the thin silk of her dressing-gown about her slender body.

'There's no need. We'll be dashing away almost immediately, I imagine. You don't even have to meet him if you'd rather not, you know.' She was apprehensive that the sparks would fly if they came face to face, in fact. For they'd never been able to meet in the old days without rubbing each other up the wrong way. They'd never pretended to like each other, even for her sake.

'Oh, I don't mind meeting him. But don't expect me to be nice to him,' Leonie said bluntly. 'I might not even manage to be civil if I start thinking about the way he treated you!'

Claudia headed for the front door as the bell suddenly pealed throughout the flat, loud and insistent and demanding. It was unmistakably Eliot's ring—she remembered it from former times! It caused her heart to lurch with painful remembrance.

He was unexpectedly on time. The clock was chiming the hour just as she opened the door to him with a slightly heightened colour in her cheeks.

'Hallo, Eliot.' Her smile was cool, admirably composed. 'Come in. I'm ready.'

'So I see.' He looked down at her, taking in the elegant coil of red-gold hair and the careful make-up and the stylish and very pretty suit with slightly amused and appreciative admiration. 'You look charming.' Before she could draw back or check him, he bent to kiss her cheek.

His easy confidence made her fume but she stifled the irritation rather than start the day on the wrong foot. But he was so damnably sure of himself, so infuriatingly arrogant. Just as he'd always been.

'You're surprisingly punctual,' she said dryly, marvelling that she was so unmoved by this man's dark good looks and engaging smile and the warm touch of his lips on her cheek. It seemed that there was nothing so dead as the ashes of a burned-out love.

'I've turned over a new leaf,' he drawled, dark eyes dancing. 'Didn't I tell you so?'

'I've lost the habit of believing the things you say, Eliot.' Claudia led the way into the room where Leonie was still sitting over her leisurely breakfast. 'There's fresh coffee if you'd care for a cup. You remember Leonie, of course.' It was light, throwaway. She'd told him that she shared the flat with a friend who was also a nurse. She hadn't prepared him for this meeting with a former adversary and she noted the annoyance and swift displeasure that narrowed his eyes.

'Lord, yes! Of course I do!' He made a quick recovery and held out his hand to her friend, smiling. 'Nice to see you again, Leonie. It's been a long time.'

He didn't attempt to kiss *her* cheek, Claudia observed with dry amusement. No doubt he was deterred by the militant spark in the grey eyes and the hostile tilt to that rounded chin.

'Four years,' Leonie said, pointedly. Her tone was cold. The outstretched hand was ignored. She didn't believe in compromise. 'Not a day too long and several years too soon, as far as I'm concerned.'

Eliot laughed softly. 'You haven't changed.'

'I don't suppose that you have, either.' It was silky and very sweet and heavy with unmistakable meaning.

'Oh, I've improved beyond recognition,' he returned in the lazy irony that was disarmingly attractive. 'I'm only half as black as I'm painted these days.' He smiled at the girl who looked back at him with such determined dislike.

Leonie was startled to discover that she reacted to the warmth of his smile and the hint of laughter in the dark eyes. She'd forgotten the good looks, the charm of that slow and slightly mocking smile, the charisma of the man—or perhaps she'd never felt their impact until that moment.

For the first time, she almost understood how Claudia had fallen so deeply in love and stayed there all these years. For there was something about Eliot Hailey that unexpectedly tugged at her own emotions and she was astonished by the involuntary response to a man that she'd been loyally prepared to hate in the name of friendship.

'Do you want coffee, Eliot?' Claudia broke into a confrontation that seemed to have undertones that she remembered only too well from earlier days.

She hoped he hadn't come back only to hurt and humiliate her all over again with the help of her best friend. Then she remembered that he couldn't hurt her any more and that it no longer mattered what he did or which woman was briefly important to him. She was free of the bonds of loving that had held her too tightly for too long!

'No time, I'm afraid. I'm parked on a double yellow line and we ought to be making a quick getaway, Claudia. I expect traffic wardens still have a gift for turning up when they are least welcome!'

'I'll just get my bag.'

In the bedroom, snatching a moment to check her hair and make-up one more time, Claudia heard the murmur of their voices through the open door. Were they making polite conversation—two people who'd never bothered to be polite to each other in the past? Or were they venturing towards a more meaningful relationship? Maybe they were merely talking about his new job and Leonie's beloved babies that would force them into close contact in the future.

She was sure that something had sparked between them—and it hadn't been the old animosity. Well, they'd have plenty of opportunity to meet on *and* off duty if they wished. She wouldn't really be surprised if Leonie had taken one of her swift fancies to a man she'd always disliked in the past. She was mercurial—and Eliot was a sensual opportunist. It was a dangerous combination.

Going down in the lift, Eliot was silent as he studied her with a slight smile quirking his mouth. They stood close in the confines of the small lift and Claudia was suddenly and disturbingly aware of the effect of his potent masculinity—a strange prickling at the nape of her neck and a tingling excitement rippled through her body from head to toe. It was a very physical reaction to a very physical magnetism and she'd never known anything like the unmistakably sexual response to his nearness and the way he looked down at her with that intent glow in the depths of his eyes.

She'd always admired the lean, good looks, the slow smile, the dancing dark eyes, even though they didn't seem to have the power to stir her senses as they should. She'd loved him, heart and soul, but her body had never quickened at his touch or known the urgency of passion or the ecstasy of fulfilment. Now, without warning, she came alive with a new awareness and understanding, a sexual awakening that vibrated in every fibre of her being—her first-ever experience of the stirring tide of desire!

Shaken, almost shocked, she dragged her gaze from those compelling, hypnotic eyes and pretended to check the contents of her slim clutch bag of cream leather for her door-key, desperate to conceal that shattering impact on her unsuspecting emotions. Her sexuality had lain dormant all these years. Now she was engulfed in the flame of passion and it took all her strength of mind not to turn into arms that had once been so eager to hold her, not to invite with lips and willing body the urgent lovemaking that had completely failed to arouse her to response when they lived together as man and wife.

Such feelings were totally out of place in the present circumstances and must be stifled, she told herself firmly. How could she want a man that she no longer loved! How could she even think of wantonly melting into his arms in long-overdue passion? At the same time, she was relieved to discover that she *could* respond like any normal woman to the physical magnetism of a very attractive man—even if the awakening had come much too late to save their marriage. It was marvellous to know that she wasn't some frigid freak of nature, after all!

'You didn't mention that you shared a flat with Leonie,' Eliot said coolly. He disapproved, for Leonie was likely to throw a spanner in the works and enjoy doing it, he knew. She'd always disliked him intensely.

Claudia glanced at him. 'Didn't I?' Her tone was slightly too casual. 'It seemed a good idea and I was grateful that she suggested it when I gave up the flat. I couldn't afford a place on my own and I didn't want to go back to my parents. I'm just as independent of them as ever, by the way,' she added pointedly. 'I still don't run to Daddy when the bills need paying.'

He put a hand to her elbow to guide her from the lift, unaware that his touch sent a shaft of tingling delight hurtling through her to ignite the flame of desire more fiercely. She reacted as though she'd been stung, jerking from his hand. He pretended not to notice the instinctive recoil but it didn't please him.

'How are your parents?' he asked lightly as they walked the few yards to his parked car. 'Even in darkest Africa, I read the occasional news item about my famous in-laws.'

'Very well—and busy, of course. Currently appearing in a play at the Atheneum,' she said pleasantly, over-looking his readiness to claim connection with her well-known parents, Warren and Daphne deFrise, while choosing to forget that he was married to their daughter. But she hoped that he wouldn't mention the fact to any of his new colleagues at Pat's. It was another secret that she'd kept for a very long time from most of her fellow-nurses.

'I must make a point of seeing it.'

'I expect I can arrange seats for you.' Claudia felt compelled to make the offer.

'Only if you promise to go with me.'

'You aren't serious!'

'Yes, I am. Why shouldn't I want to take a very attractive woman to the theatre—and why shouldn't you want to be escorted by a very attractive man?' he asked.

Claudia was torn between amusement and irritation. She shook her head. 'Take someone else, Eliot. You won't have any problem finding a substitute for me. You never did, after all,' she reminded him, pausing by the Mercedes and waiting for him to unlock the passenger door.

Reaching to switch on the ignition, Eliot was very conscious of the woman at his side. He remembered the haunting perfume of her hair and skin teasing his senses and it seemed to banish the years between past and present, so that it was natural and easy to feel the glow of admiration and the stirring of desire for his lovely wife.

He wanted her suddenly, passionately, with a mixture of old and new feelings.

He hadn't expected her to be still in love with him, of course. He knew that she had no reason to remember him with tenderness. He'd been moved by curiosity rather than sentiment to look her up when he heard that she was still at Pat's and he'd been relieved and pleased to learn that she'd got on with her life and scarcely missed him. It had eased the conscience that had pricked him occasionally during the past four years.

Struck anew by her glowing good looks, the strength of character and the warmth of personality that had originally attracted him, he'd abruptly realised that he'd missed her more than he'd known. Courting his own wife was a novel idea but he felt it was probably doomed to failure. She was no longer a starry-eyed innocent to be rushed into love but a mature and level-headed woman who didn't seem to need him or anyone else for her happiness. She'd obviously found contentment and fulfilment in her job and nursing had taken the place of marriage in her life.

Claudia glanced at him curiously. He seemed tense, a nerve throbbing in the lean cheek, his hands gripping the steering wheel so tightly that the knuckles were white against the tan of his skin from the African sun. It was impossible to read anything in the inscrutable dark eyes. Once, she would have known intuitively if he was angry or depressed or merely preoccupied. Now he was a stranger and there was a wall between them that she didn't particularly want to break down. For she felt it might be safer and wiser to see very little of him.

Sensing her gaze, he turned to smile, suddenly, disarmingly. 'Sorry. I was just working out a plan of campaign,' he said lightly. 'I've addresses of some likely flats and I think we'll look at one or two and then do something about lunch. The first is just around the corner. Too near for your liking, perhaps?' The car slid smoothly away from the kerb.

He rejected the first and second flats on the merest of pretexts, Claudia felt. Both were suitable and reasonably priced service flats, ideal bachelor pads for a busy doctor. The third was on the top floor of a terraced house in a turning just a stone's-throw from the hospital. Several of the rather shabby houses in the narrow street had been converted into flats that were popular with Pat's staff because they were convenient and cheap. Claudia knew that Trevor lived in one of them but she wasn't sure of the address.

They climbed the steep staircase and Eliot produced a key and ushered her into a well-furnished living-room that was light and spacious. Claudia explored, throwing open doors to reveal a small but well-equipped kitchen, an adequate bathroom, two bedrooms. The flat seemed to be still occupied and she didn't linger in any of the rooms. Going back to Eliot, she found him testing the comfort of the deep sofa, entirely at his ease, long legs outstretched.

'Well, what do you think? Tailor-made for me, isn't it?'

Claudia was doubtful. 'Isn't it rather too big for one person? These older houses can be expensive and time-consuming to run, too.'

He shrugged. 'I like plenty of room and old houses. And maybe I'll look around for someone to share the place with me.'

The gleam of mischief in his eyes left her in no doubt of his meaning. 'Someone to cook and clean and warm your bed, I suppose,' she said tartly, unamused.

He inclined his dark head, smiling. 'You told me to find a substitute for you,' he answered.

'You obviously prefer this flat to the others. You seem to be very much at home in it already.' Deliberately, Claudia changed the subject, ignoring his words.

'Oh, I am.' His smile deepened. 'I moved in yesterday, actually.'

The cool words and the confident smile sparked her to sudden anger. 'Oh, that's typical! We've wasted an entire morning looking at flats that you didn't even want! I've better things to do with my time even if you haven't!' She caught up the bag she'd laid on a table. 'Well, I don't have to waste the rest of the day with you!'

He moved fast, reaching the door fractionally before she did. 'Don't go! Aren't you going to help me to unpack the rest of my things and turn the place into home with a few womanly touches? And I thought I could rely on you to cook the steaks for our lunch,' he said maddeningly.

She glowered. 'I won't be used, Eliot. Not by you—not any more! Unpack, cook lunch, wash out a few socks too, perhaps? What do you think I am, for heaven's sake? The silly little fool that you married!'

He shrugged. 'So I'll cook the steaks.'

She thrust him away from the door, unmoved by the twinkle in his eyes. 'I hope you enjoy them!'

'Don't run out on me, Claudia,' he said gently.

Her chin went up. 'Why not? You did it to me!'

He frowned impatiently. 'I didn't bring you here to rake over the past.' He strode to a window and stood looking out, his back to her. Claudia hesitated, wondering why she didn't just walk out and be done with him. Everything about him infuriated her in that moment. The proud set of that dark head, the arrogance in every line of his tall frame, the too-attractive profile. 'There's a splendid view of the river from here,' he said unexpectedly. 'Come and see . . .'

Drawn by a ripple of amusement in the deep voice, Claudia reluctantly moved to his side and found, just as she'd suspected, that the 'splendid view' was the merest glimpse of a slate-coloured Thames between tall buildings in the distance. 'There's a better view of chimney-pots,' she said coldly.

'You have a discerning eye,' he approved, amused. The dark eyes rested on her thoughtfully. 'This flat was offered unexpectedly and I leaped at it. I didn't tell you because I didn't want to lose this day with you. Oh, I've handled it badly, I know. Put it down to inexperience. Trying to redeem myself with my own wife is something new for me.'

Claudia looked at him, sceptical. 'Is that what this is all about? Trailing me round on a wild-goose chase and luring me to this flat on false pretences?'

'Not to mention suggesting that you cook the lunch,' he agreed, sympathetically. 'That was the last straw.'

Claudia smiled involuntarily. But she was puzzled, wary. She wasn't sure what he wanted from her and hoped he didn't have a possible reconciliation in mind. For that was utterly out of the question. She'd never trust him again.

'I told you it was over—and it is,' she said tautly.

Eliot nodded. 'Of course it is. This is a new beginning for two very different people,' he told her, coolly confident.

Claudia stiffened. 'I'm all in favour of a new beginning. But not with you. I hope I can learn from my mistakes!'

His eyes narrowed. 'You've learned to hate, it seems.'

The quiet words made her feel oddly uncomfortable and almost guilty that love had died when she'd once sworn that it would live for ever. 'That's too strong a word,' she refuted swiftly, defensively. 'I don't hate you.

I just despise you. You're selfish and ruthless and arrogant and convinced that your charm and a clever way with words will always get you what you want.'

'He smiled. 'So it does,' he said softly. 'And I want *you*, Claudia. Very much . . .'

It was so unexpected that shock tingled all the way down her spine and the blood swept through her veins in a torrent of icy fire. She stared at him, incredulous. The smile in his dark eyes turned slowly to a glow of intent and he reached for her, his arm going about her to catch her to his hard chest. Claudia opened her mouth to utter an involuntary, angry protest and was silenced by the warm seeking of his lips on her own.

She'd forgotten his kiss, the power and the passion in his embrace. She'd forgotten the ardour and the urgency in the way he held and kissed her. She had never known the tumultuous tumbling of her senses and the wild clamour of her body in response and she clung to him for a moment in a kind of enchantment. Then she broke free, deeply disturbed, trembling with the emotion that she hoped he would believe to be fury.

'Don't make love to me, Eliot,' she said fiercely. 'I don't care for it.'

'Some things never change, do they?' he mocked, his dark eyes glittering with angry dismay.

For one heady moment, he'd thought that she was responding to the fire that burned so fiercely in him—in the way that he'd so desperately wanted in the days of loving and shared dreams and high hopes. But he'd been mistaken. She hadn't changed in the most important way of all to a man as sensual as himself.

She was still the ice maiden that he'd married.

CHAPTER SEVEN

TREVOR walked into the ward halfway through the morning. Claudia's heart gave a little thump at the sight of the surgeon, tall and blond and good-looking and really rather dear to her, even if she was still a long way from loving him.

She wasn't at all sure that she'd ever love any man again, in fact. She did know that nothing remained of her feeling for the man she'd married and she could only marvel at the leaping excitement that Eliot had evoked in her so unexpectedly and so strangely. It was a physical weakness that she meant to fight with all her might, for if any man benefited from the sudden and welcome thawing of her frigidity, she was determined that it shouldn't be Eliot.

She rather hoped that it would be Trevor. He'd telephoned her twice during the weekend, once on Saturday morning when she was out with Eliot and again on Sunday when she had gone to spend the day with her parents.

Like herself, he'd been off duty and he'd apparently hoped that they might meet. Leonie had given her the message that he'd phoned on both occasions.

Not knowing his telephone number and not sure of his address, Claudia hadn't been able to contact him. Now, she was hoping for the chance of a private word.

She'd been expecting him, looking out for him, while she set her nurses to various tasks and busied herself with preparing the patients who were due to go to theatre that day. Two of them were on Trevor's list, a partial gastrectomy and a nephrectomy, and she knew he would be in to visit and reassure them one more time before they went for surgery.

He pushed through the swing-doors when she was with the young man who was listed for the removal of a kidney. Pausing for a word with Lesley Wilmot at the desk, he glanced in her direction and nodded. Then he began to walk the length of the ward with a nod for one man and a word for another and a smile for the pretty Carol Gray as she passed him with a covered receiver on her way to the sluice.

Claudia smiled at the anxious young man. 'Here's Mr Page. He'll be pleased to tell you anything that you want to know, so don't be afraid to ask.' She looked up to meet the surgeon's blue eyes, unexpectedly cool. 'Good morning, Mr Page.' The smile she sent him conveyed the warmth that etiquette barred from her formal tone.

'Good morning, Sister.' He acknowledged her with a brief nod and turned to his patient. 'How are you feeling, Mr Sullivan? Anxious, I daresay. But I expect Sister has told you that there's nothing to worry about. It's a straightforward operation and you'll be up and about in a few days.'

'Mr Sullivan would like you to explain things more fully so that he knows exactly what it is that you're going to do and how it will affect him,' Claudia said quietly. She knew he was rushed. She also knew that he'd always find time for something as important as calming the fears of a nervous patient.

She was too well-trained to show by even the flicker of an eyelid that she'd sensed the distance in his manner and felt the dismissal in the way he'd turned away from her to speak to his patient. Had he already heard about Eliot? It was only too possible, she thought nervously.

News travelled at the speed of light via the hospital grapevine!

'My pleasure,' he said lightly, drawing up a chair and sitting down beside the young man as though he had all day to talk to him. 'Supposing you ask me some questions, Mr Sullivan. I'm the man with all the answers.'

Wryly, he wished that were true as he turned an attentive ear to his patient's anxious queries and did his best to reassure him. He knew a great deal about surgery. But at times he felt that he knew absolutely nothing about women, particularly when it came to Claudia.

She seemed to be avoiding him. Two or three times she'd been absent from the ward when he'd arrived for his round. Maybe by chance, possibly by design. On occasions when she *had* been available to accompany him about the ward or to discuss the treatment or progress of a patient, he'd sensed a slight constraint and wondered if she was regretting the evening she'd spent with him outside the clinical evironment of the hospital. It certainly hadn't worked out the way that he'd hoped, but at least they'd parted with a slight promise of better things.

He'd been surprised when Leonie told him that Claudia was spending the day with her parents in Hampstead when he'd telephoned on the previous afternoon. He hadn't known that she had any family in London and it depressed him to realise just how little he actually knew about the girl who'd become rather too important to him. She was reserved to the point of shutting him out of her personal life altogether and he wondered if he'd ever get to play a real part in it. Perhaps he ought to cut loose while he still could—before he began to love her in earnest!

Claudia entered the injection that she'd just given Mr

Sullivan on his chart and ran a careful eye over the notes of routine PTR and blood pressure checks carried out by junior nurses. Listening with half an ear to the surgeon's quiet voice as he talked to the young man, and observing the gradual relaxation of Mr Sullivan's tension, she thought how much he was liked and trusted by his patients.

She liked and trusted him, too. He was reputed to be a flirt but she didn't think he encouraged any girl to fall seriously in love or to dream dreams or weave plans for a shared future. Like many ambitious surgeons, it was unlikely that he had any thought of marriage at this stage in his career and probably avoided the commitment of loving. He was probably just the man she needed at this time. She wanted to feel that she mattered to someone but she didn't want the trauma of love. She might find it surprisingly easy to go into Trevor's arms and forget all about Eliot, the painful past and the rather doubtful future.

But that *would* set the grapevine humming with wildly exaggerated speculation about the ward sister who had a doctor husband and surgeon lover on the same staff, she thought dryly. Matron would *not* be amused! Eyebrows would be raised at every level of the hospital hierarchy. The juniors would no longer have any respect for her either as a person or as Sister Fleming. She would become the butt of bawdy comment and the probable target for every amorous male in a white coat that she chanced to encounter in a quiet corridor.

She knew that some of her fellow-nurses had managed to enjoy discreet affairs with doctors or medical students and even the occasional consultant without falling foul of Matron. But she was a married woman. Once Trevor knew that about her, it was not very likely that he'd run the risk of damaging his reputation and possibly his career by becoming further involved with her—on or off the ward. He wouldn't even want her for a friend, she thought ruefully, rousing from reverie as the surgeon got to his feet.

'You can lead a normal life with only one kidney. It's in excellent order and should see you through to ripe old age,' Trevor declared confidently.

The patient looked relieved. 'Well, that's a load off my mind, anyway, Doc. Thanks very much.'

'I'll ask Sister to send her prettiest nurse along with you to hold your hand. That should take your mind off everything else. It always works for me,' Trevor said lightly.

Claudia smiled. 'I think I can spare Nurse Gray to go down with Mr Sullivan,' she agreed, smiling at the young man who brightened at the mention of the popular junior. Patients always referred to going *down* for surgery, although operating theatres were situated on the top floor of the hospital. Some of the very junior nurses hastened to set them right but they soon learned that it was a waste of time. Patients liked to cling to their convictions.

At a nod from Trevor, she returned the chart to its hook and stood waiting to fall in step with him as he moved away from the bed. With a final word for Mr Sullivan, he came to join her and they walked down the ward towards the elderly man who was the other patient on his list for that morning.

'How is Mr Kostapolous? Still depressed?' It was casual. Trevor had noticed the way that a ray of sunshine, slanting through a window, found the golden lights in her gleaming hair and illumined her oval face to a kind of beauty. His heart contracted with a rush of emotion that really had no place on a hospital ward.

'Yes, I'm afraid he is. He knows that he's very ill and

he isn't expecting to come through today's surgery. I wasn't on duty yesterday but I'm told that there was a very noisy and tearful scene with his relatives during visiting hours and it upset the whole ward. So I think it will be better for all concerned if we nurse him in a side ward when he comes back from theatre.'

'Sadly, we can't do much for the poor old boy but make him as comfortable as possible for the short time that's left to him,' he said with genuine concern and compassion, dragging his thoughts from the woman by his side to the patient who needed his surgical skill. 'Did you manage to have a word with the son about the possibility of transferring him to a hospice?'

'I took him into my office and explained the situation to him on Friday. The family isn't happy about it, I gather. But housing conditions apparently make it impossible for his father to be nursed at home, even with the back-up of the local GP and community nurses. So at least the son is reconciled to the idea and I'm relying on him to persuade Mr Kostapolous. I've mentioned it once or twice, very casually, but he gets very distressed, I'm afraid.'

After more than thirty years in England, the old man's knowledge of the language still deserted him in times of stress. Nurses who tried to do things for him or offer a few words of comfort and reassurance were frequently greeted with a torrent that Lesley Wilmot loudly declared to be all Greek to her.

It wasn't unkind humour. Every nurse had to retain the ability to smile in the midst of so much sickness and suffering. A sense of humour was an absolute essential although it often puzzled patients and relatives to hear a burst of laughter from sluice or kitchen or clinical room—and sometimes it upset them, too. A nurse's emotions were closely involved with her patients if she was a good nurse, Claudia believed. None of her nurses were hard or insensitive or uncaring, although the layman believed it at times because a nurse had to adopt a veneer of light-hearted impersonality and seeming detachment to protect herself and the patients. A nurse who wept in sympathy or recoiled from certain sights was no good to the patient or to Pat's. However she might feel, she had a job to do and it was essential to do it well and cheerfully.

Mr Kostapolous was huddled in a tight ball beneath the bedcovers, attempting to shut out the reality of the surrounding ward and the sights and sounds that reminded him too vividly of the imminent surgery that he dreaded.

Trevor moved to the head of the bed and bent over the elderly Greek. Claudia couldn't hear the quiet words but she observed their almost immediate effect on the sick and frightened man. Trevor seemed to inspire new hope and a kind of courage in his patients. She'd noticed it many times. He was worth a dozen Eliots, she thought with sudden passion.

Some minutes later, they left a less apprehensive Mr Kostapolous sitting against a nest of pillows and waiting with calm resignation to meet his fate. As surgeon and sister neared the ward doors, the trolley for the mid-morning drinks was trundled out of the kitchen by Nurse Murray.

Claudia glanced at Trevor with a hint of uncertainty. 'I wonder if you can spare me a few more minutes? There is one other thing that I'd like to talk over with you.' She hoped she didn't sound quite as diffident as she felt.

He looked at his watch, the automatic reflex action of a man with too many demands on his time. 'A few minutes is about all I can spare this morning.' He didn't mean to be brusque but he had a heavy list to get through and that didn't take into account the possibility of any emergencies that might arise during the day. 'It won't wait, I take it?'

Having mentally girded her loins to tell him the truth, Claudia didn't want to postpone the opportunity. 'It *is* rather important.' She smiled at him. 'How long does it take to drink a cup of coffee?' From earliest training days, she'd known that there was one offer that a busy doctor never refused.

'That sounds like bribery and corruption—and very nice, too.' Smiling, he followed her into the privacy of her office.

Like every overworked doctor, Trevor knew the value of relaxing at odd moments that offered themselves and he sank gratefully into a chair and leaned his blond head against its padded back, studying Claudia as she poured the coffee and noting the deftness of her slim, well-groomed hands.

She performed the task with the quiet and graceful economy of movement of the well-trained nurse. At times, he thought that she might have made a good surgeon. She seemed to have the right degree of dedication and the essential cool-headedness and single-minded attention to detail combined with very dexterous hands. She was the kind of nurse that any doctor would be glad to have at his side in an emergency. She was the kind of woman that he increasingly felt he'd like to have at his side for the rest of his life.

He shook off the momentary thought as she handed him the cup of coffee with a slight smile. 'Thank you, Sister.' The formality was a habit. And it protected them both from unwelcome gossip. There were too many watching eyes and listening ears to note the slightest familiarity between doctor and nurse.

Claudia tried not to feel that the formal words and

tone put her at a deliberate distance. 'I'm sorry I missed your calls,' she said lightly, introducing the personal.

'I ought not to have expected you to be spending precious free time at home. I gather you were on a family visit.' He was casual. He didn't want her to feel that he was probing.

She nodded. 'I had lunch with my parents. Sunday is really their only free day at the moment. That's one of the drawbacks to working in the theatre, of course.'

'The theatre?'

'Oh, the other kind,' she qualified quickly, smiling. 'Show business. My parents are actors—Warren and Daphne deFrise. I daresay you've heard of them.'

'Who hasn't?' Trevor looked at her thoughtfully. 'So I learn a little more about you, by slow degrees. I don't think you've ever spoken about your family until now.'

'Perhaps not.' It was evasive. The famous name was only one of the reasons why she'd chosen to retain her married name all these years. Claudia had broken with tradition to nurse, disliking the limelight that was the breath of life to the rest of her family. DeFrises had belonged to an adoring public for generations and they were often in the news for one reason or another. She preferred to be ordinary Sister Hailey whose private life was of no interest to anyone but herself.

'You haven't told me much about yourself at all, in fact,' Trevor prompted gently.

Now was the moment to tell him more, just as she'd planned and rehearsed. Instead, rather too quickly, Claudia mentioned a patient who was giving cause for concern because of an unfavourable reaction to a certain drug. Trevor agreed that the dosage might be reduced without impairing the effectiveness of the drug and she made a note on her desk pad.

'Now, tell me what's really on your mind,' he invited

quietly, with the warm smile that swiftly won the confidence of his patients.

Claudia capped her pen and drew a deep breath, meeting the kindly concern in the blue eyes with the directness that it deserved. She was so sure of his understanding that she didn't know why she hesitated to admit to a marriage that had ended in too-predictable failure. 'Something that I ought to have told you some time ago,' she said, carefully feeling her way along the tightrope of revelation.

'Another skeleton in the cupboard?' He smiled, encouraging, unsuspecting.

She couldn't manage a smile in answer to the gentle teasing. Her heart was pounding and she found that she was ceaselessly turning the pen in nervous fingers. She laid it down with precision. 'I daresay you'll feel that I've deliberately kept you in the dark. Like not telling you about my parents. But actually it just happens to be something that I don't talk about easily. Trevor, I should have told you that I'm married.'

The words spilled in a sudden rush and they rocked him. She saw the jerk of his hand as he set down his coffee-cup with a clatter. She saw the hardening of his blue eyes in surprise and suspicion, the abrupt tightening of his mouth. She saw trust and friendship and affection vanish from his expression and knew how much they had begun to mean to her. He'd always felt like a friend. Now, he turned into a stranger at the impact of her words. With a sinking heart, she knew that he wouldn't understand—and wasn't likely to forgive.

'*Married!*' The echo was jolted out of him. 'When did *that* happen?'

'Over four years ago.' She reached to straighten the tilting cup that threatened to overturn in its saucer. It was an entirely automatic reaction.

'*Four years!*' Trevor stared in utter disbelief, total astonishment. He thought of the warmth and sweetness that had brought him so near to loving her. He thought of the delight of holding her in his arms and the dream that he might persuade her to love him one day. He didn't want to think of her as another man's wife.

'I was nineteen. It didn't work out.' She spoke carefully, wanting him to understand. 'It's a long time since we lived together, Trevor. He . . . he found someone else.' It was hard to make the admission. It might not have the power to hurt these days but it was still painful to her pride.

'I see.' His tone was grim, uncomprehending. He didn't see at all, in fact. And he was angry that she hadn't told him the truth about herself before he'd begun to care for her. 'Why tell me now? At this late date? There were other opportunities—and better moments,' he said stiffly.

Claudia flushed at the reminder of an evening when she'd relented and gone out with him, invited his lovemaking. 'You had to know before you heard it from someone else.'

Trevor frowned. 'Someone else? Your friend, Leonie? Not very likely, is it? If she made a habit of talking about your affairs to all and sundry, everyone would know that you have a husband—and it seems to be a very well-kept secret,' he said with a touch of bitterness.

'No, not Leonie. She wouldn't tell anyone without my say-so. She's absolutely to be trusted.'

'And I'm not?' His eyes narrowed with pain.

'Oh, Trevor! It has nothing to do with not trusting you,' she said quickly, contrite.

'Well, that's how it seems to me.' He rose and headed

for the door. 'However, I haven't the time to talk about it now—or the inclination, to be frank.'

'Please don't go! There's more!'

'I don't think I want to hear any more. And I'm late, anyway.' He glanced at his watch, impatient.

'Do listen!' Claudia moved swiftly to detain him with an impulsive hand on his arm. 'I have to tell you the rest. Eliot, my husband—he's *here*! Working at Pat's. You saw us together the other day in the pub. He's Sir Hartley's new registrar.'

He looked down at her, a muscle tensing in his jaw. 'Is he, indeed? How long have you known about that, I wonder?'

'Only since last week. He came to see me, to tell me about the appointment. I hadn't seen or heard of him in four years. It was something of a shock.' The distress in her quiet voice invited his sympathy.

'Last week!' Trevor shook off her hand angrily. 'And you wait until now to tell me! It didn't occur to you that I might hear from another source that the new registrar just happens to be your husband!' He ran a hand through the thatch of his blond hair. 'I suppose you didn't care that it might be "something of a shock" to me, too?'

'I'm sorry.'

'You should have warned me from the start that wanting you was a waste of time—and a dangerous pursuit for a man in my position,' he said grimly.

'Yes. I'm sorry,' she repeated lamely, knowing that she had no defence against a justifiable rebuke. Even the most innocent of friendships with a married woman could be the cause of scandal for a surgeon and Trevor was in line for a consultancy and couldn't afford to take chances with his reputation. They'd been so discreet that she doubted if anyone knew of their friendship. But it was obvious that he would be even more discreet, much more formal, in the days to come and that the new warmth in their relationship would die an abrupt death.

'I don't know that you are,' he said brusquely. 'Perhaps you rather enjoyed dangling me on a string.' The angry words overlooked just how little encouragement she'd actually given him in the past months.

'I hope you know me better than to think that,' Claudia returned quietly.

He shrugged. 'It seems that I don't know very much about you at all.' It was pointed.

She coloured. 'I wanted to tell you—so many times. But some things aren't easily talked about, Trevor. Not by me, anyway. I've always kept my job and my private life in separate compartments and you know that I don't make a habit of talking about myself. Perhaps it's a form of shyness, or self-defence.'

'Pride, more likely,' he amended cuttingly, hand on the door. 'Everyone sees you as the capable and competent Sister Hailey, so efficient and well-organised. So no one must know that things can go wrong for you and that your private life is a mess!'

The door closed abruptly on the surgeon and his wounded pride. Claudia sighed as the telephone shrilled, demanding attention. She turned to answer it like a dutiful nurse, fighting dismay at the way that Trevor had left her, fighting a foolish impulse to run after him and ignore the demands of her work. It was Accident and Emergency, requiring a bed for a road accident victim, and she forced herself to concentrate on the voice in her ear.

She no longer wanted Eliot, her husband and now, she'd lost Trevor, the one man who might have been able to persuade her to forget the past.

She was obviously destined to spend her life as a ward sister—she might eventually get to be Matron, she thought darkly. She loved nursing, so it was strange that there was very little comfort in the thought that it might prove to be her entire life . . .

CHAPTER EIGHT

GOING to late lunch, Claudia wasn't too surprised to find the senior staff cafeteria humming with talk of Eliot, who seemed to have made his presence felt in a very short space of time. For that was typically Eliot.

He couldn't help being a very attractive man with his impressive height, lean build, distinctive good looks and the easy charm that women had always liked, of course. But he didn't have to be such a flirt. She didn't doubt that he'd been scanning the prettiest of Pat's nurses for likely conquests ever since he'd set foot in the hospital.

An admiring glance for one, a warm smile for another, a meaningful, murmured word if an opportunity offered—oh, she knew his tactics! However, she didn't care what he did as long as no one knew that she was married to him. She wondered ruefully just how long it would take the grapevine to ferret out that interesting piece of gossip.

Taking her tray to a quiet corner, she sat down at an empty table and hoped that no one would attempt to draw her into discussion of the new medical registrar. The hope was short-lived, for, within minutes, she was joined by a relief sister with a reputation for gossiping and a determined refusal to be snubbed.

She drew out a chair and sat down at Claudia's table, uninvited. 'Hi! How are things on Fleming these days? Just as busy as ever?' She didn't wait for a reply but swept on brightly. 'I suppose you know all about the new addition to the staff? The dashing Dr Hailey! Relative of yours, by any chance, Claudia? He wouldn't be a brother, for instance?' Brown eyes in a plump and pretty face sparkled with avid interest.

Claudia smiled, shook her head. It seemed that Eliot was being discreet and she was grateful. 'No. He isn't a brother.'

Louise Mottram seized on a hint of evasion in the lightly-spoken words. 'There is a connection, though?'

'Not a very important one.' It was the truth as far as she was concerned, she told herself firmly. Once, her marriage had been the most important thing in her life. Now, it played a small and very insignificant part in the life that had changed so much in four years.

'But you *are* related?' It was persistent, eager. 'That's useful.' Louise beamed. 'Do me a favour and introduce me to him, will you? I'm head over heels since I saw him this morning. He's a gorgeous hunk of man—and just my type! So good-looking—and where did he get that super tan?'

'He's been abroad. Working in Africa.' It was safe to assume that Eliot would have extensively advertised that fact, Claudia felt.

'That explains it. He isn't married, is he?' It was blatantly optimistic.

Claudia hesitated. Direct questions were more difficult for someone who hated lying. She parried the question with another in the lightest tone she could muster.

'Does he act married these days? I haven't seen him in years, but he used to be a shocking flirt.' She pushed a lettuce leaf about her plate without appetite, wishing that he'd stayed in Tanzania and out of her life. Eliot was a complication that she just didn't need. 'Where are you working these days?' she asked, hoping to change the subject.

'Out-patients. Mary Halliday's still sick, poor girl, so

I'm temporarily in charge of the paediatric clinic. That's how I happened to see your cousin. He arrived this morning for Sir Hartley's clinic. Six feet of sex appeal! One smile and we were all going down like ninepins!'

'Sounds untidy . . .' Claudia forced a smile. She didn't bother to correct Louise's careless assumption. It might simplify matters, after all. She didn't mind having Eliot for a cousin. She just didn't want him for a husband! She must warn him not to deny the false item of information that would probably sweep through Pat's like a forest fire.

Louise laughed. 'Oh, I don't think he even noticed. He was more interested in the kids. He's good with them, isn't he? Oh, I know it's his job but he has that extra touch that really counts. Just the right manner— and he's really lovely with the tinies.' Her voice softened sentimentally.

Claudia realised with a prickle of resentment that she didn't have the least idea whether or not he was good with kids. It was disconcerting to realise that she'd never known that he wanted to work with children. Wasn't it something that a loving wife ought to have known? she found herself wondering. Had she failed him in more than one way, after all?

'Meaning that he didn't hold them upside down, I suppose? I daresay he was trying to impress his new boss,' she said coolly, suddenly impatient with a weakness that, incredibly, still seemed to want to make excuses for a bad husband.

Louise looked at her in surprise, struck by the tartness of the comment, wondering what Claudia Hailey had against her handsome cousin. She'd liked the new registrar. He'd been charming and courteous but he'd had his mind on his work rather than her nurses, she'd felt. 'I think he was concerned with doing his best for the kids,' she said firmly. It was almost a reproach.

Certainly Claudia felt rebuked. Leaving her untouched dessert and half-drunk coffee, she rose from her chair, almost too abruptly. She couldn't sit and listen to a fellow-nurse singing the praises of the man that she had good reason to distrust and despise! No one but herself knew the real Eliot Hailey. He won friends and influenced people much too easily with his devastating good looks and dangerously deceptive charm. No doubt he'd have everyone at Pat's eating out of his hand within days—particularly the too-susceptible juniors!

'I must get back to Fleming. We're rushed off our feet today. Half the ward seems to be going to or coming from the theatre,' she said brightly. 'It's chaos!'

'Don't forget your promise,' Louise called after her confidently. 'I'm relying on that introduction!'

Claudia couldn't recall that she'd made any promises. She had no intention of helping Eliot to enjoy himself with a succession of Pat's nurses under her very nose, she thought bitterly, hurrying away before anyone else could waylay her with eager questions about the new doctor with the same surname as herself.

She hadn't exaggerated the situation on Fleming, after all. She got back to the ward to find that another pair of hands was desperately needed. Things had seemed comparatively quiet when she left her senior staff nurse in charge while she went for a belated lunch-break. She returned to something approaching real chaos.

Nurse Murray had been whisked to sick bay with suspected appendicitis. She'd bravely but foolishly struggled through her morning routines without mentioning the stabbing pain in her side which bent her double at intervals, nor the sickness that had finally overwhelmed her in the sluice and aroused the suspicions of a passing houseman. Staff Nurse Julie Gordon had gone off duty for the afternoon. Mr Kostapolous had come back from theatre in a critical condition and Lesley Wilmot was helping the houseman to set up an intravenous drip and attach the sick man to the machine that would monitor heart rate and blood pressure and instantly alert the staff to any changes.

Claudia's experienced eye told her that the Greek gentleman was in a very bad way and that he'd need careful nursing for the next few days. The operation had been carried out to give him only a temporary lease of life, she knew—and he had known it, too. Some patients lived longer than expected against all odds. Some simply gave up on hearing that they had an incurable disease. Claudia wondered if Mr Kostapolous would ever occupy the bed that had been promised for him at the local hospice where the nuns provided the best possible care for terminal cases.

'He's going to need constant observation if we aren't to lose him, Sister.' Trevor's young houseman was adjusting the flow of the drip that provided the patient with a steady supply of essential plasma. 'Will you arrange for a nurse to sit with him, please?'

He was slightly diffident, even apologetic, knowing that the request for a special would put an extra strain on her already-stretched team of nurses. The patient was surrounded by an array of modern medical equipment with built-in warning systems that were supposed to do away with the necessity of a nurse at the bedside, but there were still times when a doctor decided that he didn't wish a patient to be left unattended.

It was the sister's job to carry out the doctor's wishes and Claudia was brisk, reassuring and unhesitating despite the staff shortage on the ward. 'Certainly, Mr Hall. I'll see to it right away.' She made a mental note to ask

Matron for another nurse as well as the promised replacement for Nurse Murray. She prided herself on managing for the most part, but there were occasions when even the most efficiently run ward had to call for extra staff to help out with the work-load.

She moved towards the door, glancing at the staff nurse who was checking the drainage tube that led from the patient to the plastic container beneath the bed. She thought that Lesley seemed subdued, almost tense. 'Everything all right, Staff?'

'Yes, Sister. Everything's under control, thank you,' Lesley said formally, to the sound of breaking glass from the clinical room on the other side of the corridor.

'What on earth . . . !' Claudia broke off, lips tightening. The flicker of dismay in the staff nurse's face spoke volumes and it was obvious that there had been a series of small disasters during her brief absence from the ward. Claudia felt that she wouldn't need to look too far for the cause.

'All right, Staff. I'll investigate,' she said crisply. 'You'd better stay with Mr Kostapolous for the time being. I'll send a nurse to relieve you as soon as I can.' She hurried into the corridor just as a theatre porter trundled a trolley through the swing-doors.

'Afternoon, Sister. Theatre's ready for Mr Sullivan,' he announced importantly, still new enough to the job to introduce a touch of drama to the task of transporting a patient from ward to ante-room, where the anaesthetist waited.

'Very well. Just a moment, please.' The young man with the diseased kidney was drowsy from the pre-med but he probably remembered her promise that Nurse Gray should go with him to the theatre. The first-year ought to be standing by with the patient's folder. She knew just where to look for the missing junior, Claudia thought grimly, heading for the clinical room.

Carol Gray was hastily gathering up the pieces of a shattered bottle of chlorhexidine that she'd dropped in the process of laying up a trolley for a dressing. The pungent smell of the disinfecting lotion filled the small room.

Claudia surveyed the scene with grim disapproval. 'How did that happen, Nurse?' Her tone was even colder than her amber eyes. She'd been very patient with this particular nurse. Possibly too patient.

'I'm sorry, Sister. It just slipped . . .' With the back of her hand, the girl brushed a strand of fair hair from her eyes. Guilt and distress made her tone defiant.

Claudia studied the flushed face without a trace of her usual sympathy for a junior's disasters. She'd made more than enough allowances, she decided, hardening her heart. As usual, the cap that seemed to have a life of its own was sliding towards the floor. As usual, the apron was creased and grubby and just now it was splashed and stained with chlorhexidine. As usual, the black brogues were sadly in need of some polish while the pretty face wore rather more make-up than Matron approved for Pat's nurses.

Suddenly, Claudia had a mental vision of the typically male admiration in Eliot's glance for the little junior. It had entirely overlooked her total unsuitability as a nurse. Men were such fools—and especially men like Eliot who couldn't seem to see beyond a pretty face and an attractive figure!

Carol Gray was haphazard and careless and untidy and she was always behind with her routine chores because she spent too much time talking to the patients or asking questions of any houseman who had the time or inclination to indulge her passion for knowledge.

She'd been an excellent student, the star of her set in the preliminary training school and the delight of Sister Tutor, by all accounts. But the moment she was sent to work on the wards she'd seemed utterly incapable of living up to her promise. Like every sister on every ward that she'd so far graced—if that was the right word for such an accident-prone junior—Claudia doubted if the girl would finish her three-year course of training as a Pat's nurse. The thirst for knowledge was a good thing and theory was an excellent grounding, but it was practical work that really mattered in nursing.

'Things have a habit of slipping through your hands, Nurse Gray. You really must attend to what you're doing. My patients will soon feel that they might be safer *under* their beds than in them when you're on the ward,' she said coldly. 'Clear up this mess quickly. Then report to me in a clean apron and with your cap on straight!'

'Yes, Sister. Thank you, Sister.' It was a meek, automatic response. Claudia sensed a ripple of rebellion beneath the surface and made up her mind to give the girl a scolding that she wouldn't soon forget.

She stalked from the room and summoned another first-year from the sluice where she was busily packing the autoclave with instruments for sterilisation. The bored junior was delighted to accompany Mr Sullivan.

Claudia stood at the top of the ward and surveyed the two rows of demanding patients, reviewing her sadly depleted staff. The road accident victim was being prepped for emergency neuro-surgery by her remaining staff nurse, which meant that the drugs round was delayed. She went for the keys of the drugs trolley, meaning to begin the round with a much chastened Carol Gray to assist her.

But before she could do more than unlock the trolley,

the neurosurgeon walked into the ward, accompanied by the registrar and houseman and half a dozen students. He'd been called to perform the emergency craniotomy and he wished to examine the man and give lengthy and detailed instructions on after-care. Claudia slipped the keys into her pocket and hurried to greet him with the deference due to a senior consultant.

While he explained the surgical technique to his students, she hovered dutifully, sending the staff nurse to do the drugs round with a second-year. Carol Gray had failed to show her face since she'd been left clearing up the mess in the clinical room. An elderly patient who had been transferred from the geriatric ward for a throat operation began to bang on his locker with a spoon, unable to call out and stubbornly refusing to grasp the niceties of the bedside buzzer. Claudia frowned and beckoned to a nurse who was hurrying with a receiver for a vomiting patient.

'Attend to Mr O'Leary as quickly as you can—*and take that spoon away from him*,' she said, quietly but firmly.

She listened attentively and politely to the drone of the Professor's voice while the bustle of the ward went on about them. Out of the corner of her eye she saw Mr O'Leary doing battle with the nurse. He was obviously reluctant to part with the spoon, which he saw as his only means of getting attention from the busy staff. A physiotherapist was having trouble in persuading a post-op patient that the recommended exercises were essential to his recovery. Finding them painful, he was loud and foul-mouthed in protest, causing the girl to blush and Claudia's mouth to tighten with annoyance.

A registrar came into the ward, very late for his round, and there was no senior nurse free to accompany him. He stood by the ward desk, frowning, tapping an impatient foot and casting impatient glances in Claudia's direction. She caught her staff nurse's eye and the nurse reluctantly closed and locked the drugs trolley and left the drugs round to attend to him.

The first of the visitors were peering through the windows of the swing-doors, eager to invade the ward as soon as she gave permission—and sooner if they could get away with it, she thought coldly. A straggle of patients were making their way between their beds and the bathrooms or the day-room in readiness for the visiting hour.

Fleming was never quiet but somehow it usually managed to be orderly under Claudia's calm handling. Today was different. For the first time, she felt that the reins were slipping through her hands.

The Professor and his retinue went away at last. The registrar finished his round and went with a curt nod for her that made her fume. She went to look for Carol Gray and found her in the office, clean and tidy and outwardly repentant. She gave the girl a short, sharp telling-off that almost reduced her to tears, one final warning, and sent her to relieve Lesley in the side ward. Then she turned her attention and her energies to other matters.

By the time that order had been restored by dint of hard work and careful delegation and the visitors had been admitted with their flowers and bulging carrier bags, she was glad to escape to her sitting-room and close the door on the bustle that she'd set in motion.

She sank into a chair, kicked off her shoes and reached for the still-unread *Lancet*—and was abruptly reminded of Eliot, sitting on her desk, swinging a long leg and idly glancing through its pages. She tossed it aside impatiently. The last thing she wanted was any reminder of Eliot.

He'd unsettled her by coming back. She'd been

getting on so well without him. She just didn't want him around to stir up the muddy waters of the past, she thought resentfully. She leaned back and closed her eyes, trying to relax the knot of tension in the pit of her stomach. Then, hearing the unmistakable sound of Eliot's deep voice outside the door, she sat up stiffly, every nerve protesting.

He walked in without even the pretence of a preliminary knock, smiling, much too sure of himself, tall and dark and impressive in a formal grey suit beneath the white coat. The dashing Dr Hailey! The husband she fervently wished that she'd never met, let alone married! Claudia glowered at him.

'So here you are,' he said, smiling down at her just as though he didn't recognise the frost in her amber eyes. 'Sitting with your feet up while your terrified minions scurry up and down the ward.'

'I hope they are scurrying to good effect,' she said crisply, trying to slip her feet unobtrusively back into her shoes. 'Or I shall have something sharp to say to them when I get back to the ward!'

She felt vulnerable and unprofessional without her shoes. Just as if she'd let down the entire race of hospital sisters by being caught in her stockinged feet in the privacy of her sitting-room. For sisters weren't supposed to be human beings with feet that ached—or with hearts that sometimes yearned for something more than caring for patients, dancing attendance on doctors, chivvying junior nurses or writing out routine reports.

One shoe remained elusive. Eliot stooped to retrieve it from beneath her chair. Then he reached for her slender, black-stockinged foot and cradled it in his strong hand for a moment before easing it into the sensible brogue. Claudia experienced a strange rush of tingling excitement that swept from head to toe in response to the casual, almost absent-minded service, and the blood stormed into her oval face.

'There you are, Cinderella.' He didn't appear to notice her confusion or her heightened colour. He straightened, smiling. 'I didn't know you could be so fierce. Now I understand why your nurses are so afraid of you. You've turned into a dragon, breathing fire . . . the scourge of defenceless patients, hard-working nurses and well-meaning doctors. All due to frustration, of course. You need a man in your life, my love,' he drawled.

'I'll look around for one,' she said, sharp with irritation at the too-easy and utterly meaningless endearment.

'You could do worse than settle for the one you married,' he suggested lazily, dark eyes resting on her with an enigmatic gleam in their depths.

'Don't be absurd! What do you want, Eliot? Don't you have any work to do?' She rose impatiently. He'd ruined her few precious moments of relaxation and she might as well return to the ward, she thought crossly.

'I'm on my way to Matthew. But I wanted a word with you. I've just been told that we're cousins, Claudia. You can't hope to get away with that, you know. Truth will out,' he said dryly.

She shrugged. 'It wasn't my idea and it isn't my fault if people leap to the wrong conclusion. You don't have to confirm it. Just don't deny it.'

He raised a sardonic eyebrow. 'Ashamed to own me as your husband?' It was amused, mocking.

She looked daggers. 'Should I be proud to be married to you?' The hurt and the bitterness of the past suddenly welled with new force and overflowed as scorn.

Eliot didn't flinch from the look in her amber eyes.

'Given the chance, I believe I could make you proud of it,' he said, coolly confident.

'You won't get *half* a chance! And no one has to know the truth about us, surely? It isn't anyone's business but mine!'

'And mine,' he reminded her smoothly.

'It suited you to forget it for years. Why does it suddenly suit you to remember? Does your new boss think you have a dutiful wife who cooks your meals and brings your slippers and tells you twice a day how wonderful you are? Well, I'm not prepared to play that part again, Eliot. Not for you or any other man!'

He regarded her thoughtfully, eyes narrowed. 'What makes you think that I want you back as a dutiful wife? The mere thought fills me with horror. You should wait to be asked before you hurl refusals in my face.'

Claudia coloured vividly. It seemed she'd leaped to a wrong conclusion of her own and she felt foolish. 'As long as you know that it's a waste of time to ask!'

'I'll remember.' He turned to the door, paused. 'I haven't met your blond boyfriend yet, by the way. Page, isn't it? Known him a long time, have you? I mustn't ask how well, I suppose?' His smile indicated good-natured, almost indifferent acceptance of the probability that they were lovers.

Claudia didn't trust that smooth and smiling attitude. He'd never liked to be thwarted and if he'd suddenly and surprisingly decided to want her back, despite that cool denial, he might use any means to get what he wanted. Including a threat to slander the reputation and injure the career of a fellow doctor.

'Not well at all,' she said firmly. 'We just work together. There hasn't been any man in my life since you walked out, Eliot. You can check with Leonie if you wish. She'll tell you that it's true—and tell you what she thinks of you into the bargain!' she added.

'Oh, I believe you. After all, it can't be easy to find another man like me,' he mocked. 'And you were never the type to settle for inferior goods.'

He closed the door so speedily behind him that *The Lancet*, hurled at his head in sudden exasperation, struck the wooden panels and fell harmlessly to the floor.

CHAPTER NINE

THANKFULLY going off duty at the end of a very trying day, Claudia saw Trevor in conversation with a staff nurse in the main hall of the hospital. He was smiling, relaxed, very personable. The girl was slim and pretty and warmly encouraging in the way that she smiled back at him, obviously pleased and flattered by the notice of the good-looking blond surgeon.

Passing them, Claudia nodded and smiled with carefully impersonal, incurious friendliness and walked on, wondering why she was drawn to the kind of man who liked women too well. Eliot had never been able to keep his hands off other women and ought never to have married. Trevor was reputed to be something of a flirt and he'd possibly only regarded her as a challenge because she kept him and every other man at a distance. Now, disappointed, he'd already dismissed her and was in hot pursuit of someone else, she decided, heart sinking slightly.

She pushed through the heavy glass doors and emerged into a drizzle of rain. She began to make her way down the stone steps, drawing her cloak about her to keep out the damp chill of the evening that seemed to penetrate to the very heart of her.

'Sister! Sister Hailey! Just a moment . . .'

Surprised and pleased, Claudia turned, ready with a smile for the surgeon as he swung down the steps to reach her side. 'Good evening, Mr Page,' she said formally. But her amber eyes were warm with a hint of relief that he hadn't dismissed her entirely, after all.

'I haven't had a chance to get back to Fleming but I've been hoping to see you,' he said, without preliminary. 'You're rather late going off duty this evening, aren't you? I thought I must have missed you.'

Her heart lifted at the implication that he'd been hanging about the main hall in the hope of catching her on the way from the ward. 'I've been waiting for a patient to come back from the theatre,' she explained. 'It was rather an interesting case. A craniotomy. We don't get many of those and I wanted to know how it went.' She didn't add that she'd chosen to work late rather than hurry home to the likelihood of an empty flat and a lonely evening.

'Oh, yes . . . Hammond's case. I heard about that. I gather it was successful.' He put a light hand at her elbow in automatic courtesy as they continued down the steps to the pavement. 'I was hard on you this morning,' he went on, rather abruptly. 'But you did spring it on me, you know. Out of the blue.'

Claudia bit her lip, not looking at him. 'There didn't seem to be any other way to say it—and you had to know as soon as possible. Before you met Eliot or heard about him—and found out the truth.'

'It explains a good deal about you that puzzled me,' he said frankly. 'I've always felt that you liked me but you kept me so firmly at arm's length that I just couldn't understand it. Now, of course, I know that you had a very good reason for turning me down so many times. Persistence finally paid off to some extent and I'm tempted to believe that if it wasn't for the wedding-ring that you never wear, we might have been on extremely close terms by this time.'

Claudia smiled at him. 'Possibly.'

His answering smile came and went. 'I just wish that you'd told me sooner, Claudia.'

'So do I,' she said quietly.

They stood together at the foot of the steps, blond surgeon and distinctively attractive sister wrapped in her navy cloak against the rain, jostled by the motley crowd who surged towards the hospital entrance with the advent of the evening visiting hours but apparently unaware of anything but each other.

A sleek Mercedes came to a halt at the traffic lights of the pedestrian-controlled crossing outside the famous hospital. The driver's attention was caught by the couple and he glanced at them briefly and then looked again, intent, eyes narrowing abruptly. A smile flickered about his mouth but his grip on the steering wheel tightened to whiten the knuckles of deeply tanned hands.

The traffic-lights changed to green and the last of the pedestrians scurried to safety on the pavement. The Mercedes slowly moved forward and almost immediately turned into Hoyle Street. Neither the car nor its driver had been observed by Claudia or her companion.

'This man—Hailey.' Trevor found it too painful to refer to the man as her husband. He looked down at her soberly. 'I haven't met him yet but I'm told that he seems to be good at his job—and a charmer. The kind who makes an instant and lasting impression, apparently. People are talking about him at every turn.'

'So I gather.' Claudia was rueful.

'You say that you haven't seen him in years . . .'

'That's perfectly true,' she said quickly, on the defensive.

'I'm not doubting you. I'm just wondering . . . he walked out on you but you're still married to him, Claudia. Does that mean that you're still in love with him, too?'

'*No! No, I'm not!*' It was swift, involuntary protest.

'Sure about that?'

'Quite sure,' she said firmly.

'Then perhaps you should think about getting a divorce.'

Claudia nodded. 'Yes. Perhaps I should.' Her heart was thudding. She wondered where he was leading—and felt that she knew.

'If you were free . . .' He broke off. 'Let's walk on,' he said brusquely, noticing the curious glances of a couple of nurses who came down the steps in their direction. 'This is too public for private conversation. You're going home, I take it?'

'Yes. But should you be seen with me . . . in the circumstances?' she said.

He frowned. 'The circumstances are not of my making,' he reminded her quietly.

'No. I'm sorry. That wasn't fair.'

Trevor walked by her side, silent. Claudia stepped out briskly, using the drizzling rain as a reason for hurrying but really wanting to put an end to their encounter as soon as possible. There was no need for him to explain anything to her, she thought with painful understanding. She knew exactly what was in his mind.

'You must know how I feel about you,' he said stiffly, after several moments of searching for the right words and failing to find them. 'But you also know that it's difficult for me, in my position, to go on seeing you. I can't afford even the hint of a scandal. If you didn't work at Pat's—if you weren't a sister . . .' The words trailed off as he shrugged, not with indifference but from heaviness of heart.

'It's all right, Trevor. I know what you're trying to say and I do understand,' she assured him gently. She hadn't expected anything else but it was like him to try to let her down lightly. He was so kind, so caring.

'Do you?' He glanced at her and away again, eyes

troubled. 'I'm in love with you, Claudia. It tears me to pieces to think of you as another man's wife. If I'd known . . .' He smiled a twisted smile. 'I'd still be in love with you, I guess.'

Someone darted across the road, dodging the stream of traffic, and almost collided with them as he reached the pavement. Instinctively, Claudia moved closer to Trevor and he put a protective arm about her, glowering at the man who brushed past them and hurried towards the hospital entrance. He hugged Claudia briefly and then withdrew his arm, too conscious that eyes might be watching and tongues wagging. As senior surgeon and the ward sister, they were obviously familiar figures and from the hospital windows even the busiest nurse could snatch a moment to look out at the High Street with its steady flow of pedestrians and traffic.

'I never wanted this to happen,' Claudia said, subdued.

'Nor did I,' he admitted frankly. 'And it isn't going to be easy, pretending that I'm not interested in you when I am, very much. I may overdo it at times, Claudia. It won't mean that I've changed or lost interest. I shall still be caring. Hurry up and get that divorce and I can stop pretending and start making up for the way that bastard treated you.'

Claudia made allowances for a very natural jealousy, but she still flinched. It was well deserved, but she still didn't like to hear Eliot abused. There had been faults on both sides, after all. She hadn't been such a wonderful wife.

'Don't come any further with me, Trevor. You're getting quite wet.'

She had her cloak and the navy outdoor cap to protect her from the drizzle that was rapidly turning into a downpour and she could run the last hundred yards if necessary. She was young enough to be unconcerned with her dignity and she was no longer on duty.

He reached for her hand and squeezed it so hard that she winced with the pain of his grip. Then he released her and turned and strode away, heading for Hoyle Street without a backward glance. Claudia looked after him, almost relieved. Not knowing what to say to him, she'd been anxious to escape. She'd known that he was fond of her. She'd tried to warn him against loving her. She was moved by the unexpected declaration of his feelings but she wasn't ready to love again and she couldn't give him any promise for the future. It might not be any different once she was finally free of the millstone of her marriage. She liked him so much. But that wasn't loving . . .

True to his word, Trevor was distant when they met again, a few days later. He was very much the surgeon, aloof and impersonal, exchanging the merest platitudes with the ward sister, formally discussing the needs and problems of his patients. If he hadn't said that he was in love with her, she could never have suspected it from his courteous but decidedly cool attitude, she thought, relieved rather than dismayed.

Life was easier, smoother, without the threat of emotional disturbance or demands. She was almost grateful for the circumstances that compelled Trevor to be discreet and to put their friendship on ice for the time being. She really didn't want to be involved with him or anyone else at the moment.

Just now, she was content to give her all to nursing, she decided, settling down to some paperwork when he had finished his round and left the ward. She wrote a few lines in her neat, careful hand and then glanced up, frowning, as a shadow fell across her desk. Her nurses had plenty to do and she wasn't expecting any interruptions.

'Oh, it's you!' she exclaimed involuntarily, startled into irritation by the sight of the dark-haired doctor who lounged in the open doorway, studying her with that infuriating gleam of mocking amusement in his dark eyes. 'What do you want now?'

Eliot raised an eyebrow. 'Not a very warm welcome for the love of your life. Try again, Mrs Hailey,' he suggested lazily.

Claudia stiffened. 'Don't call me that!' she said sharply. 'Do you want the whole world to know?'

He smiled, shrugged. 'I'd happily shout it from the roof-tops. What man wouldn't, married to someone like you? Beautiful *and* clever. You're the one who insists on making a secret of it.' But he came into the room and closed the door. 'Don't worry. No one heard. The ward is a hive of activity and there isn't a soul within earshot,' he comforted.

She wasn't comforted. She wasn't flattered by the easy and meaningless compliment, either. She looked at him coldly. 'Walls have ears in this place. What is it, Eliot? What do you want? People will soon start to gossip if you keep coming here to see me. Medical staff have no business on a surgical ward.'

'I'm irresistibly drawn by the desire to see you, my love,' he told her smoothly. 'And I don't mind who knows it. Cousins may visit each other, surely?'

She flushed. 'Don't make life difficult for me, Eliot. It's bad enough that you had to come back from the wilds of Africa or wherever. I never wanted to see you again!'

'Liar,' he said softly, very gently, turning the epithet into the most tender of endearments.

She met his eyes, warm and teasing. Her own were

cold and hard and very angry. 'Believe what you like!' she snapped. 'It really doesn't matter.'

'Being a woman, you hoped I'd be back on my knees, begging to be forgiven, declaring that I'd thrown away all my happiness and swearing that I'd never loved anyone but you.' He smiled suddenly, disarmingly. 'Did you forget that I never could admit to a mistake without choking on my pride?'

Damn his pride—*and* his perception! That was exactly what she *had* hoped for too many years. Now, she was thankful that she no longer loved him—that his sneering words couldn't hurt and that his indifference suited her present frame of mind so well.

'Of course I hoped along those lines for a few months,' she returned coolly. 'But hope doesn't spring eternal, whatever the poets might say, and *I'm* proud, too. I stopped loving you and wanting you back a long time ago.'

'Very wise. I was never worth it. Isn't that what everyone tells you?'

Claudia suddenly lost patience. 'Look, say what you came to say and then go, please. I haven't time to talk about the past *ad nauseam* and there isn't any point!'

'I came armed with a dinner invitation but I seem to have chosen the wrong moment.'

'Dinner!' She stared at him blankly.

'Tonight, I thought,' he said smoothly. 'You agreed that we should see each other occasionally as friends. It seemed a friendly thing to do to book a table for two and ask you to join me.'

She shook her head. 'No.'

'A previous engagement?' He smiled, questioningly.

'No. I just don't feel very friendly where you're concerned,' she said bluntly, with truth.

'That's what I said. It's the wrong moment.' He

shrugged. 'Never mind. I'll take someone else to dinner.'

'Good idea.' Indifferent, Claudia bent her head over the papers on her desk. If she acted busy and ignored him, perhaps he would take the hint and leave.

Certainly he turned to the door and actually had a hand to it when it opened abruptly and Trevor walked into the office.

'Sister, I seem to have walked off with Mr Bevan's discharge certificate . . .' He broke off as Eliot moved into view. 'I'm sorry, Sister. I didn't know that you were engaged,' Trevor said stiffly.

It was an unfortunate choice of words, in the circumstances. Claudia didn't need to glance at Eliot to know that devilish merriment lurked in the dark eyes and to anticipate the obvious retort.

'The lady's married, in fact. But I think you must know that,' he said. He held out his hand. 'Page, isn't it? I'm Hailey.'

'Yes, I know.' For a moment, Trevor looked as if he meant to ignore that outstretched hand. But ingrained courtesy combined with the rigidity of medical etiquette proved too strong despite the hostility that lay heavily between them. He shook hands, very formally. 'How do you do?' He turned to lay a slip of paper on the desk in front of Claudia. 'Sorry about that, Sister. I found it among my papers.'

'Thank you. I hadn't missed it yet.' She sent him a very warm smile. He looked back at her so coldly that her heart sank—and then rallied as she realised that he was maintaining a frigid pretence for Eliot's benefit and their mutual protection.

The surgeon went as quickly as he'd come. Eliot observed the slight flush in Claudia's lovely face without pleasure. 'I wonder what you see in that cold fish. Like to like, I suppose,' he commented harshly. Words and tone dismissed the nonsense that there was nothing between them.

She bridled, but she didn't mean to be provoked into unwise words. 'Like everyone else, I have a great deal of respect and admiration for a very able surgeon,' she declared stiffly. Eliot uttered a very rude word, a crisp and expressive reaction to the pompous remark. The colour flamed in her cheeks. 'I think you'd better go.' Coldly furious, she rose to her feet, quite angry enough to eject him forcibly if necessary.

'Before I sully the innocent ears of your nurses?' He smiled, unrepentant. 'Tell me, Claudia, does respect and admiration stretch to include a little loving when you're both off duty?' The inference was obvious.

'No, it doesn't!'

'He isn't in love with you?'

Her innate honesty baulked at the instant denial that his mocking tone merited. But he was much too perceptive for comfort. 'We certainly aren't lovers,' she compromised.

He laughed, softly. 'I'll take your word for it, my love. Not much red blood in his veins, I imagine—and only ice in yours. You make a fine pair!'

'Excuse me, Sister . . .' Carol Gray tapped lightly on the open door. 'Staff said to remind you about Mr Perry's injection.'

Claudia welcomed the interruption and the timely reminder. She hadn't forgotten Mr Perry, of course. It was just that Eliot and Trevor together had temporarily crowded the man from her mind. 'His insulin? Yes, I'll see to it. Thank you, Nurse.'

She wondered if the girl had overheard any of the conversation. She looked harassed and preoccupied, like most juniors, and she sped away as soon as the message was delivered as if a dozen chores were pressing. But the glance she'd shot at Eliot had been keen and comprehensive and she'd probably hurried off to whisper with Jilly Wayne in the sluice, Claudia thought dully, remembering her own early training days and the flutter and the gossip whenever a good-looking doctor came into the ward.

Removing her organza cuffs, she laid them carefully in a drawer of her desk. Then she began to roll up her sleeves in readiness for the task of preparing the regular injection of insulin for Mr Perry, a diabetic recovering from an operation for a prolapsed disc in his back.

Eliot watched her for a moment and then stretched his tall frame like a man stirring from sleep. 'I must get along to Matthew. I'm rather concerned about one mite who's wasting away before our eyes—so far we can't find the cause. The poor little chap's too weak for surgery, I'm afraid. But we shall lose him if we don't operate, anyway. It's a problem.'

'If you're so concerned about your patient why are you wasting time with me?' Claudia demanded tartly, refusing to be impressed by the warmth of compassion in his voice.

'Why, indeed?' he countered lightly. 'I shall get a much warmer welcome on Matthew. I wonder if Leonie is doing anything this evening?' He sauntered off, smiling.

He was infuriating and arrogant, Claudia thought crossly, filling a hypodermic syringe from an ampoule of insulin and checking the dosage with the automatic conscientiousness of the trained nurse. She scorned that smooth reference to Leonie with the contempt it deserved, of course. He might make a pass but he wouldn't get anywhere with her straight-talking friend!

Her confidence cracked slightly as Leonie rushed

from bedroom to bathroom and back again that evening, in the throes of getting ready for an obviously important date.

'Someone special?' Claudia asked, carefully casually. She had hung her blue sister's dress in the wardrobe and slipped gratefully into the coolness of a kimono that her mother had brought her from a recent visit to Japan. The delicate tracery and vivid colours of the embroidery on an ice-blue background made it a delightful garment and Claudia loved it, although it was slightly too small and the heavy silk had a tendency to slide away from her tilting breasts with every movement.

'Not exactly. Someone I've known for a long time and just haven't got around to dating until now.'

Claudia wondered if she only imagined a kind of conscious evasion in her friend's reply. Leonie was usually so forthcoming about her boyfriends. 'Dinner date, is it?' She sat on Leonie's bed, filing a chipped finger-nail, while Leonie hustled into a pretty blue and white spotted silk dress.

'He's taking me to one of those exclusive Soho restaurants, apparently. He's the type who does things in style. Table for two in a secluded corner, flowers for the lady—and violins on order, too, I expect.' She laughed, slightly flushed with excitement. 'All very romantic!'

Claudia smiled, reassured. It certainly didn't sound like Eliot! 'Any chance that you'll come home with a ring on your finger?' she teased.

A shadow touched her friend's pretty face. 'No chance at all,' she returned, with a brittle tone. 'He happens to be married.'

The smile froze on Claudia's lips. 'That doesn't sound your style.' It was concern rather than reproach.

'No, it doesn't, does it?' Leonie checked the contents of her bag, carefully not meeting Claudia's eye. She'd always been so rigidly disapproving about such affairs. The sound of a car horn in the street below sent her moving swiftly for the door. 'That's my man! He won't come up, of course, in the circumstances!'

As the flat door closed on her friend, Claudia sat very still, struggling with suspicion. It couldn't be Eliot—and yet Leonie had been unusually ill at ease and reluctant to talk about her date. Of course, she would be embarrassed if she was dating Eliot after all she'd said about him throughout the years. But he was a very attractive man and her friend had always been susceptible to the tall, dark and handsome type, Claudia reminded herself wryly.

It was dreadful to pry, to spy on Leonie, but something stronger than scruples drove her to the bedroom window that looked down on the narrow street. One glance told her all that she'd needed to know. A sleek and too-familiar Mercedes was parked outside. Obviously Eliot's car, even if she couldn't see the number plate from this distance.

She didn't *mind*, of course. But she was troubled for Leonie. She couldn't interfere but she knew as no one else did that Eliot just wasn't to be trusted . . .

CHAPTER TEN

THRUSTING the thought of Eliot and Leonie as a couple firmly to the back of her mind, Claudia decided to have a bath and wash her hair before she prepared a snack meal and settled down to watch television for what remained of the evening.

She went into the bathroom and turned on the taps and threw in a handful of her favourite bath salts. She was removing the pins that kept her long hair in its neat and shining coil when she heard the doorbell. It rang so loudly and so insistently that she wondered if the caller had been trying to attract attention for some minutes. The running water might have stifled the sound of the bell.

Wondering if it could be Trevor, needing to see her for all his insistence on discretion, she hurried to the door—and opened it to Eliot, laden with flowers and cartons and a bottle of wine.

'You! I thought . . .' She broke off abruptly, not wanting him to know just what she had thought. That odd little surge of emotion that swept through her at the sight of him couldn't be relief—or delight, she decided. For she wasn't at all pleased to see him on her doorstep, so sure of himself, so sure of a welcome.

So handsome, too, in formal suit and crisp shirt and fashionably narrow tie, his black hair gleaming and his dark eyes smiling down at her with obvious amusement for her astonishment.

'You wouldn't come out to dinner. So I've brought dinner to you,' he announced.

'You never could take no for an answer,' she said coldly. But she stood back to let him enter.

He presented her with the bouquet. She put it on the hall table, unimpressed, far from pleased by the gesture. *Red roses for love*, she thought crossly, hating the way he'd always mocked the sentiments that other people held dear. She felt like throwing the elegant, long-stemmed and undoubtedly expensive flowers at his handsome head.

'Put them in water, Claudia,' he urged lightly. 'It's a warm night and they probably need a drink as much as I do.'

'Too warm a night for playing games. You aren't staying, Eliot. I'm hot and tired and I'm just about to have a bath.'

'Then you'll need me to wash your back—and you can't expect me to eat two lots of pizza and drink all this wine by myself.'

She resisted the disarming warmth of eyes and smile and lazy words. 'I don't know why you brought them— or what you're doing here!'

'I can't keep away from you, my love,' he told her, with a low and mocking laugh.

Claudia was growing used to the meaningless and often-used endearment. It was one that he'd never used in the days when she'd confidently believed herself to really be his love, she thought ironically. She laughed, slightly scornful, impatient with his nonsense. 'You surely don't expect me to believe that!'

'Of course. Why shouldn't I want to see you, to be with you? You are my wife,' he returned lightly, smoothly.

'You haven't wanted to remember *that* for too many years!' But she took the cartons of food and carried them into the kitchen and he followed her with the wine and stored it in the tall refrigerator to cool, as much at home as if he was a frequent and familiar visitor to the flat.

Briefly, Claudia left him to turn off the running water, giving up all ideas of relaxing and luxuriating in the fragrantly scented bath and the lazy evening that she'd planned. Heaven knew what Eliot wanted, but she just wasn't the type to turn him away—and he knew it, she thought grimly.

'I saw Leonie on her way out. I knew she had a date, of course.' His deep-set dark eyes suddenly twinkled with a hint of mischief. 'Did you think she might be hurrying to meet me, Claudia?'

'No. Why should I?' She wouldn't give him the satisfaction of knowing that his parting shot earlier in the day had been so effective. She met his eyes, shrugged. 'Leonie has too much sense to be impressed by you. She remembers you too well!'

She left the room and came back with the sheaf of roses, too tender-hearted to let their beauty wilt and die on the hall table, no matter what she felt about the giver. She took a tall crystal vase from a cupboard, filled it with water and began to arrange the lovely flowers with her deft and skilful hands.

Eliot watched her, silent and thoughtful. The last rays of the setting sun fell across her slender figure in the silk robe and caught the gold in her glorious hair as it framed her oval face and cascaded to her shoulders in richly luxuriant waves and tumbling curls. She was lovelier than she seemed to know, stirring his body and touching a core of need deep within him that he hadn't even known to exist until he'd met her again after the years of separation.

His hand moved involuntarily to touch a bright curl of her hair and he checked it. He mustn't rush his fences or he risked falling in the first furlong, he thought suddenly.

Winning had become the most important thing in his life and he suspected that Page had a head start on him.

The slight movement attracted Claudia's attention. She glanced at him and frowned, observing the slight pallor beneath the tan, the tiny beads of sweat on his brow and a hint of tension in his tall, lean frame. He'd been ill quite recently. Had he returned to work rather too soon and found the long and demanding days as a hospital doctor more exhausting than he'd remembered?

Maybe he was simply too warm in the formal suit— and he was certainly overdressed for an informal evening spent with an estranged wife. Had he dressed for a very different kind of evening and then come along to the flat on impulse, stopping for food and wine and flowers *en route*? But where on earth had he bought flowers at short notice when all the shops were closed?

She leaned to open the kitchen window as wide as possible although there wasn't much of a breeze in the still air of the hot summer night.

'You might as well take off that jacket if you're staying,' she said abruptly. 'You must be much too hot in those clothes.'

'Yes, I am . . .' He spoke absently. Her sudden movement had opened the kimono to reveal the lovely curve of a bare breast. The ache of desire was suddenly sharp in his loins and her beauty caught at his heart with unexpected force. 'You're sensibly dressed for a heat wave,' he approved, schooling that painful wave of emotion. 'I like that thing you're wearing. It has a hint of eastern promise!'

Sensing his interest in the shape of her body, Claudia suddenly remembered that she was naked beneath the slithery silk kimono. She drew it closer about her slender figure and knotted the tie more firmly, pointedly.

'It's Japanese,' she said crisply, resenting the slight stirring of excitement that the admiration in his eyes and the teasing but meaningful words evoked. Newly awakened to her own sexuality, she was conscious of the beginning of desire in him and she wondered if he was aroused by her femininity and the remembrance of past lovemaking. His potent masculinity was certainly triggering her to a response she had never known in the past. And she felt determined that he shouldn't know it.

'Very attractive,' he murmured, moving closer to admire the intricate and colourful embroidery of the kimono's design. Very gently, his long fingers began to trace the threads of the flowers that trailed across her shoulder.

The womanly scent of her was sweet and warm and disturbing, teasing his senses and causing longing to sweep over him in a flood. It took every ounce of resolution to keep from catching her close to the heart that had so unexpectedly begun to love all over again, but in a very different manner.

Claudia stood very still, tingling from head to toe at the touch that set her flesh quivering and the blood racing through her veins. She knew she ought to thrust him away in swift and contemptuous rejection of the passion that she sensed in him. It was so foolish to quicken in response and be tempted to turn and slide her arms about him and lift her face for his kiss! The least hint of encouragement would be fatal. Give him a smile and he'd seize a kiss on the strength of it. The merest response and he'd be trying to sweep her into bed. Loving didn't come into it as far as Eliot was concerned. Sex had always been an appetite to be satisfied in the arms of any woman he fancied—and maybe he'd find a degree of spice in making love to the wife who'd long since ceased to be a wife in anything but name. Claudia had no intention of allowing it to happen!

With an effort, she remained unmoving and apparently unmoved while his quickened breath was warm on her cheek and his fingers moved slowly and sensuously from her shoulder to the slope of her breast. She found herself waiting with a kind of breathless impatience for his hand to reach and curve about her in a lover's caress. Molten fire in her loins was robbing her of all resistance, all caution.

Wildly, she longed for his kiss, his embrace, the ardour and urgency of lovemaking that had once left her completely cold but now seemed to hold a promise of the kind of heaven to be found in a man's arms. The heaven of sexual delight and fulfilment, the power and glory of passion between man and woman. The heaven that she'd wondered if she would ever know with any man.

Eliot's hand stilled, hovered above the taut swell of her breast beneath the thin silk. Claudia caught her breath and her body arched unconsciously—she almost leaned against him in impulsive invitation. Desire throbbed, heady and insistent.

Abruptly, he moved from her side, his hand dropping. Glancing at him, Claudia saw the tension in his jaw and the glow of impatience in the dark eyes although he smiled his slow and rather mocking smile. She was flooded with relief even while her wilful body clamoured in disappointed protest. She realised that he hadn't sensed the fierce tide of wanting that had held her captive for those few, threatening moments. Her reputation for being an iceberg had stood her in good stead!

With the gradual quietening of her senses and the

return of caution came the renewed conviction that it would have been disastrous to melt into his arms. Even if she was still married to him!

He went into the other room and she heard the chink of a bottle on glass as he helped himself to a drink from the array on the sideboard, left-overs from one of Leonie's parties. With her heart still beating much too fast, high in her throat, Claudia put the last of his roses carefully into the vase and carried them through to the living-room. Eliot was standing with his back to her, apparently scanning the titles of some books on a shelf, and she saw him raise his glass and down the amber contents as though he badly needed the stimulant of the whisky.

She frowned, faintly troubled. He'd never been much of a drinker and she wondered if he'd acquired the habit in the past few years. She knew so little about him these days. He was so strange, so unpredictable, so changed from the man she'd once loved so much and thought she knew so well.

'Make yourself at home,' she said lightly, setting down the vase and then crossing the room to the door of her bedroom, anxious to change out of the too-revealing kimono. 'Put on some music or switch on the television or find something to read. It will only take me a few minutes to dress.'

He turned to look at her, eyebrow raised. 'Why bother? You look charming and you needn't stand on ceremony with me, Claudia. I *am* your husband, after all.'

She smiled coolly. 'You seem to have dressed for dinner. I'll return the compliment.' She closed the door with an irritated snap that banished his attempt to remind her of former intimacy, wondering why he had to speak at every turn of something she would prefer to forget. Did he get a kind of perverted pleasure from constant references to their relationship?

She whisked through the range of clothes in her wardrobe, searching for something suitable, and took down a cream chiffon dress, a favourite with its finely pleated bodice and long, filmy sleeves and the elegant frills at neck and wrists. It was much too good for Eliot but she would feel both cool and confident, she decided. With the dexterity of practice, she swept her gleaming hair into a top-knot of curls and secured it with ivory combs. A touch of lipstick, a little perfume . . . she looked at her reflection with suddenly sober eyes and wondered if she was dicing with danger.

Why on earth hadn't she shut the door in Eliot's face when she saw him on the doorstep? What could they possibly have to give each other at this late date—except a brief hour of meaningless magic, perhaps? Eliot wasn't to be trusted not to take prompt advantage of a momentary weakness and she certainly wasn't sure that she trusted the emotions that he stirred so swiftly and so strangely without even trying.

She returned to him. The sound of a haunting melody, sweet and low and achingly familiar filled the living-room. It was a ballad that had been high in the charts when they married and thus a favourite at the time. They'd danced to it at their wedding, so much in love, so confident for the shared future. For four years, Claudia hadn't been able to hear it played without choking anguish.

Now, she felt that he'd deliberately chosen to hurt her with its poignant words of the love she'd once known. She was irritated all over again by his mocking attitude to the sentiment that had been a very important part of her life, however little it had meant to him.

He was relaxed in an armchair, head thrown back

against the cushion, eyes closed. He looked so tired and dispirited that Claudia was unexpectedly touched by concern. She didn't like the way her heart moved in her breast or the absurd impulse to put out a hand to touch him in swift reassurance. He didn't deserve her compassion, and affection for him was a thing of the past, she told herself firmly, blaming the music and the memories it threw up for that brief melting.

The record ended abruptly with a jump and a squeal that was due to a flaw in the pressing of the disc, the jarring note that she'd always deplored and he'd never seemed to notice. Eliot opened his eyes. 'So it *is* the original,' he said. 'Something survived the years, after all.'

'It's about all that did.'

'Why do you keep it? To play on anniversaries?'

'I've no reason to celebrate anniversaries,' she reminded him tartly.

'This year will be different,' he promised, coolly confident.

'I doubt it. Is the wine sufficiently chilled, do you think? I'm ready to eat.' It was light, dismissive. She wasn't interested in his promises for the present or the future, she thought coldly. She hoped that by the time their next wedding anniversary came round, she'd be celebrating their divorce!

She was busy in the kitchen for several minutes. When she carried in the steaming plates of pizza, she was surprised to find that he'd laid the table with the red mats and napkins and silver cutlery and crystal glasses that she and Leonie kept for special dinner parties. He'd obviously explored the sideboard to good effect! He'd found tall red candles in a drawer and their leaping flames were reflected in the bright silver of the holders and the polished top of the oval dining-table. He'd taken one of the long-stemmed red roses from the vase and laid it by her place and he was surveying the results of his handiwork with obvious satisfaction.

Claudia stared. Then a gurgle of involuntary laughter rose to her lips. 'Oh, Eliot! Slightly overdone for take-away pizza and plonk, surely!' she exclaimed.

'Beauty demands a gracious setting,' he said quietly, very simply, drawing out her chair with a flourish that underlined the compliment.

She sank into it, oddly shaken. The vibrant warmth of his deep voice, the glow in his dark eyes and the romance that he seemed to be trying to introduce into the evening were so unexpected and so uncharacteristic that she was bewildered.

He poured the wine and raised his glass in a toast. 'To the future . . . whatever it may hold for us,' he said lightly.

Claudia hesitated. Then she nodded. 'The future,' she agreed, knowing that they weren't likely to share any part of it. She leaned forward to touch her glass gently to his and added on a sudden, warm impulse, 'I *do* wish you well, Eliot—despite everything!' She drank a little of the wine and set down her glass, smiling at him.

He nodded. 'Thank you. Things certainly seem to be moving to my advantage at the moment. The new job, the flat, finding you again . . .' It was too smooth, too confident.

Her smile fled and her fingers tightened abruptly on the slender stem of her wineglass. How like him to assume too much from a momentary impulse! He was so insufferably conceited and so damnably sure that she still felt a lingering fondness for him that would sweep her into his arms all over again if he should choose to want her!

'I'm not part of your future,' she warned sharply,

spelling it out for him. 'We've outgrown each other, Eliot!'

He looked at her levelly. 'The girl outgrew the boy and became a woman,' he agreed. 'A very lovely woman.' His strong fingers closed over her hand and the glow in his eyes compelled her to look at him, warily. 'The boy that I used to be never seemed to have the time or the patience to thaw the ice in you, Claudia. I wonder if the man might succeed where he failed.' He took her hand to his lips and pressed a kiss to the throbbing pulse in her slender wrist.

'If you're asking me to go to bed with you, the answer is no!' She whisked her hand from his hold before the flame of passion lurking behind his smile kindled the spark of her own unwelcome desire.

He sighed. 'You never used to be so blunt, my love.'

'I considered your feelings too much. When did you ever consider mine?' she demanded, even more flatly.

'You never used to say no to me, either. Not that you ever said yes with any enthusiasm, of course,' he swept on, mockery gleaming in his dark eyes.

Claudia flushed. 'Do you really expect to act the husband just when it suits you?' Ice tinkled in her tone.

'Even a bad husband has some rights,' he declared unabashed.

'You forfeited that one—and all the rest when you left me.' She looked at him with hard, angry eyes. 'I've had second thoughts, Eliot. I've decided that I *do* want a divorce. As soon as possible.'

He picked up a fork and began to eat, unconcerned. 'Just as you wish. Start proceedings in motion as soon as you like.'

'I should have done so years ago!' She was slightly taken aback by his indifference. She'd half-expected argument, protest, perhaps even persuasion. It was a relief, of course. At the same time, she was almost piqued that the things he'd said, the way he'd looked, the clever impression he'd given of renewed interest and affection had only been part and parcel of his mocking attitude to their marriage.

'Maybe you didn't have an incentive until now.' He smiled, disarmingly. 'Page pressing you to get rid of me, Claudia? Have I suddenly become an embarrassment?'

'It has nothing to do with Trevor,' she said firmly.

He shook his head at her in amused reproach. 'You shouldn't lie to me, you know. I've seen you together. The man's in love with you and you're flattered. But don't make the mistake of rushing into another disastrous marriage.'

Her chin tilted. 'I've no intention of rushing into anything.'

'Except divorce.'

It had a final sound, the death knell of a marriage, public admission of failure by two people who'd once shared love and hope and dreams. But when nothing was left of those sentiments but cold ashes then surely they should be set free to find a new and perhaps more lasting happiness?

Claudia chased a portion of pizza about her plate, making a pretence of eating. She had no appetite for the food, no desire to drink his wine, no pleasure in his company. A kind of guilt weighed heavily on her spirits, although she hadn't hurt and disappointed him, been unfaithful to him, walked out on him. She'd been a loving and loyal wife for too many years. So why should she feel a persistent and uncomfortable conviction that she'd failed him badly?

'How was your patient . . . the little boy with the marasmus?' Doctors were always pleased to talk shop and she was desperate for a change of subject.

'He died this afternoon.'

Eliot replenished the wine in their glasses. The reply was cool, matter of fact, impersonal. But Claudia thought she saw the glimmer of pain in his dark eyes. No doctor liked to lose a patient, of course. Leonie had said that he was very involved with the children in his care on Matthew and that they responded to him wonderfully well, even the tiny babies. The unexpected approval from someone who'd always disliked and distrusted him bore out the other things that Claudia had heard about him in the short time since he'd joined the staff of Pat's.

'I'm sorry,' she said quietly, a little ache in her breast for the dead child and the doctor who'd been unable to save him. 'I expect it was a blow to you.'

'It made me question the point of the training and research and bloody hard work of the past eight years,' he said, almost angrily. 'One comes to expect babies to die from lack of nourishment in East Africa. It's a shock when it happens in a London hospital with all the latest equipment and know-how and the best possible doctors.' He shrugged. 'Maybe I'm not a good enough doctor. I couldn't do anything for him.'

'What could you do in just a few days?' She was quick with her comfort, generous with her understanding and sympathy.

'That Oates hasn't been able to do before me?' He smiled wryly. 'Perhaps I thought I'd come up with a solution and make everyone sit up and take notice of the brilliant new registrar. Maybe my pride's taken a knock and I'm more concerned with losing accolades than losing a patient.'

'People *are* taking notice. Everyone says that you're a good doctor, an asset to the staff. I've heard some very complimentary things about you, in fact.'

'For all the wrong reasons.'

It was said with a hint of impatience that Claudia found oddly endearing. 'For the right reasons, too,' she said firmly. 'You're very good at your job, you're wonderful with children, you've slipped into place at Pat's as though you've always belonged and you're universally liked. Isn't that an accolade worth the having?'

'If I'm such a great guy, why are you divorcing me?' His dark eyes questioned her gently.

'You may be a marvellous doctor. But you're the worst husband in the world.' Her smile took the sting from the words.

'Then we should stay married. For you're the worst wife in the world. We obviously complement each other. Two halves of a perfect whole!' He leaned to kiss her, hard and fleetingly, full on the mouth . . .

CHAPTER ELEVEN

THE MEMORY of that kiss lingered, mocking and meaning-less though it had undoubtedly been. Going about her work on the ward, dealing with the routine paperwork, attending to patients, delegating her nurses with her brisk and effective efficiency, Claudia kept remember-ing the warmth of Eliot's mouth on her own, the sudden tilt of her startled heart and the leap of longing to know his arms about her in a once-familiar and now too-disturbing embrace.

Fortunately, she'd kept her head, laughing at him in a way that couldn't possibly have betrayed the weakness that he would swiftly have turned to his advantage. The remainder of the evening had been spent with him in remarkable amity, considering all the circumstances. It was almost as if her insistence on a divorce had laid a kind of foundation for friendship in the future. Their paths would obviously continue to cross while they both worked at Pat's. They'd fallen impulsively in love, mar-ried and parted—all within a matter of months. But they'd never had time to be friends, to discover if they liked each other or had anything in common but the bond of marriage.

He'd been a young, overworked, over-anxious doctor who saw little of the wife whose work as a nurse at a different hospital meant that their off-duty hours seldom seemed to coincide. Head over heels in love, Claudia had been too intense and too possessive, demanding too much of the man and the marriage.

Now, older and wiser and finally able to view him

dispassionately, she wondered if she'd been in love with the man she'd wanted him to be instead of the real and very human Eliot. She wondered if she'd clung to a dream of love and marriage instead of facing the disastrous reality. She wondered if she'd ever really known the man that she'd married so impulsively. Comparing him with the man of today, he seemed to have changed so much. For the better, she admitted fairly.

Unexpectedly, she'd enjoyed his company. Perhaps it was the potency of the wine or the mellow warmth of the evening or simply the charm of an attractive and intelligent man who'd set himself to please and interest her and avoided any further hint of sexual tension or reminders of past intimacy.

Claudia had found herself relaxing, warming to him, almost liking him as they talked about Pat's, his job and her own. He'd moved her to mingled laughter and tears when he talked with warm and humorous compassion about some of his youthful patients and she'd observed at first hand the surprising and obviously genuine love and concern for children that she'd never suspected in earlier days. She'd recounted some of the trials and tribulations and rewards of being a ward sister and felt that he was amused and interested and admiring.

They'd listened to music and talked books and theatre and touched, very tentatively, on family and former friends, bringing each other up to date. He'd left the flat before it grew late, parting with her on an impersonally friendly note, and she hadn't seen or spoken to him since.

That was a week ago, Claudia mused, busily detaching the electrodes of the machine that had carefully monitored Mr Kostapolous since his operation. The elderly Greek was doing very much better than anyone had expected and no longer needed special nursing or the sophisticated equipment that surrounded him. Being a sociable and garrulous man, used to the bustle of a large family about him, he was fretting to go back to the main ward and Claudia had promised to mention the matter to Trevor when the surgeon arrived for his round.

No doubt Eliot had been busy, on and off duty. He was settling into the new job, making friends, slipping easily into the social scene. He didn't need her, they had no reason to meet and she hadn't really expected to see anything of him. Their ways lay apart in the future, after all. Obviously accepting that fact, he hadn't been to the ward in search of her or tried to contact her. Her only news of him had been through Leonie and the grapevine.

Leonie had certainly changed her tune where he was concerned. She'd gone from having no time at all for him to a voluble respect for his ability as a doctor and an obvious liking for him as a man, Claudia thought witheringly, forced to listen to her friend's glowing accounts of *Eliot's* work, *Eliot's* involvement with 'her babies', *Eliot's* various successes. Leonie was so impressed that she forgot to be tactful, continually praising him to the wife who was no longer interested. One would suppose that Eliot was the only paediatrician at Pat's, listening to Leonie, and Claudia could only marvel that her friend didn't seem at all embarrassed by the sudden and complete change of heart towards a man whom she'd detested and distrusted ever since she'd known him.

Claudia was slightly anxious about her friend's obvious and increasing liking for Eliot, in fact. Their work brought them into almost daily contact on Matthew and it seemed that he was making full use of his opportunities to win over Leonie. His looks and charm and physical magnetism made him much too attractive for any girl's good and there was obviously far more depth to his character these days. But it didn't mean that he was any more reliable where women were concerned. Leonie was no fool, but an apparently abortive affair with one married man might have put her into the right frame of mind to encourage Eliot, Claudia felt.

It was surprising how many people hastened to tell her about Eliot's interest in Leonie. Everyone had apparently accepted the rumour that they were cousins as fact and no doubt assumed that she must be interested in his concerns. In fact, she simply didn't want to know. Nothing he did could hurt her now.

She didn't miss him any more. But it did seem that she was missing the habit of caring for him. Loving Eliot had been a part of her life for so long, thinking about him such a daily ritual for years, that the sudden absence of the emotional bond had left a void that had yet to be filled by another man.

Hearing a familiar step in the corridor and the sound of Trevor's voice as he spoke to one of her nurses, she was ready with a warm smile for the blond surgeon when he joined her in the side ward. Maybe it was unethical and incautious to show her feelings so openly, but Mr Kostapolous was drowsing on his pillows and she had impulsively taken an opportunity to convey to Trevor that he was still in her thoughts and in her heart, even if circumstances compelled them to behave like near-strangers.

'Sister.' Trevor nodded to her and took the chart from its hook at the foot of the bed. Carefully impersonal, no one could have known that his heart had lurched at the sight of her, lovely and slender in the traditional dark blue frock, silver-buckled belt clamping the tiny waist, starched cap sitting so precariously on the shining red-gold hair.

The enchanting smile had been reassuring to the man

troubled by the recurring anxiety that Hailey's return and his apparently effective charm might be erasing any fondness that Claudia had begun to feel for himself.

Trevor continually chafed against the inescapable fact that she was still married to the man and therefore out of reach of a surgeon forced to be discreet by the dictates of his profession and ambition. He wanted Claudia more with every day that passed and hated the necessary pretence that kept him from openly admitting and showing his feelings.

He looked up from the chart. 'You're doing very well, Mr Kostapolous,' he approved, raising his voice for the sleepy Greek's benefit. 'I'm sure that Sister must be very pleased with you.'

The hooded eyes lifted and fell. But not before surgeon and sister had glimpsed a gleam of satisfaction. A blue-veined hand plucked feebly at the bedclothes and the dark head on the pillow turned slightly in Claudia's direction. The man was still very weak but, despite all the odds, he was making progress and the prognosis was much more cheerful than anyone had expected when he returned from theatre.

'Now that he feels so much better, Mr Kostapolous finds it lonely in here,' Claudia said, mindful of her promise. 'I wonder if you agree with me that he's well enough to be transferred to the main ward, Mr Page.'

Trevor reached for the man's hand, automatically feeling for the pulse and studying the rise and fall of his breathing, searching for tell-tale signs of possible relapse in respiration and heartbeat and appearance. Then he nodded.

'If he feels up to the move and you feel that he will benefit from it, then I've no objection, Sister.'

Like all doctors, he knew that the ward sister was more attuned by virtue of her work to a patient's progress, problems and needs than he was from a brief pause at the bedside in the course of a rushed round. He certainly trusted Claudia to know what was best for her patients. He said so as they left the side ward together and walked along the corridor to continue the round.

'The bustle of the main ward might rouse him from that lethargy and I'd like to see him up and about in the near future. But I'm very impressed with his improvement and I'm inclined to give him rather longer than we originally felt. All my patients do well on Fleming, of course,' he complimented her.

Claudia warmed to the words, the hint of a smile in the blue eyes, the approval that almost bordered on the personal. It was reassuring. He was being so careful to protect them both from damaging gossip that she frequently had to remind herself of his promise that the pretence of indifference would only be *pretence*. For years, she'd clung to a foolish dream of Eliot. Now, she was clinging almost as anxiously to the reality that Trevor's declared love for her seemed to offer. She didn't want to lose him but she couldn't blame him if he decided to forgo the chance of eventual happiness with her and look around for someone else to love.

'I've an excellent team at the moment,' she said, giving credit where she felt it was due and generously overlooking the continued hazard of having one junior in particular on her ward. 'Bright, hard-working nurses who really care about the patients, and that's so important.'

'You communicate your own brand of caring to your nurses, of course,' he told her firmly. 'A good sister makes for a good team and a well-run ward. Matron certainly knew what she was doing when she put you in charge of a ward as busy and as demanding as this one.'

A blush touched her face at the words with their

obvious sincerity. 'It can be a heavy responsibility,' she reminded him, rather ruefully. 'Sometimes I wish that I was still just an ordinary nurse on the ward.'

'Sometimes I wish that you weren't a nurse at all,' he returned, low and impulsively. 'It makes things so damnably difficult.'

The words throbbed with unmistakable meaning but he carefully didn't look at her as he spoke. Patients had little to do but observe everything that went on around them and the ward staff were always on the alert for an unguarded remark or exchange of glances between a surgeon and a senior nurse that could be exaggerated into a promising affair.

'It does indeed, Mr Page,' Claudia agreed briskly and turned to take the handful of files from the ward receptionist who'd got them ready for the round. They'd been approaching the ward desk as Trevor spoke and she hoped that his words hadn't been overheard for they'd certainly be repeated within a short space of time, with additions. She was rapidly ceasing to care if the whole world knew that she had a husband and a would-be lover within the hospital walls. But it was obviously important that Trevor's name shouldn't be linked with a married sister by his colleagues or her fellow-nurses.

She couldn't help wondering if Trevor was inclined to be rather too cautious a lover, nevertheless—and she couldn't help feeling that Eliot would ride roughshod over convention and etiquette and public opinion and everything else in order to get a woman that he wanted. Maybe not very laudable, but it must certainly make the woman feel that she was essential to his happiness!

She understood that Trevor had to be discreet, of course. But she longed to be occasionally of more importance than his job, his ambition or what people might think and say. He was much too caring and conscientious, she knew—but wasn't that part of his attraction for her? It was foolish to compare him with Eliot, who'd always seemed so light-hearted about his work and everything else that she wondered how he'd achieved a plum post as registrar.

She'd promptly dismissed Leonie's scornful claim that he'd probably charmed his way into the job. Charm wouldn't have cut any ice with Sir Hartley or the Board of Hospital Management. So Eliot must be a much better doctor and far more dedicated than she'd ever known. Perhaps she'd always loved him too intensely to see him clearly . . .

As if he regretted that momentary lapse from his usual formality, Trevor was carefully impersonal for the remainder of the round. It didn't take very long that morning. He started with a few reassuring words for a patient who was on his operating list for that day, a man so jaundiced that a first-year had supposed him to be Chinese. Teased by her fellow-nurses and the patients, she'd pointed out in her defence that it didn't help that the man's name happened to be Ling! Despite the depression that was symptomatic of his condition, Mr Ling had a sense of humour and he'd promptly adopted his own brand of pidgin English to amuse the nurses and the patients. Having undergone a number of tests it had finally been determined that he had an obstruction of the bile duct that required surgery.

There was a final shake of the hand for the ebullient Paul Sullivan, the nephrectomy patient. He'd made such good progress that he was being sent by ambulance to the annexe in Surrey to convalesce so that his bed might be available for someone on the waiting-list for surgery.

Then Trevor moved on to praise and reassure those of his patients who weren't yet well enough to go home or to convalescence and needed cheering and encouragement. In light-hearted vein, he challenged one of the younger men with faking temperature and blood pressure readings so he wouldn't be discharged before he'd managed to fix a date with one of the nurses. The man's glance shot so swiftly towards Jilly Wayne who was doing the PTR round at that very moment that it was obvious that the surgeon's words weren't wholly exaggerated and there was a general laugh at the patient's expense.

Then, finally, he examined a post-operative patient who wasn't doing as well as he might and after some discussion of his case with Claudia, he suggested that the man should be moved into the side ward that Mr Kostapolous was about to vacate.

'There doesn't seem to be a pathological reason for his failure to respond to drugs and nursing care as he should. So perhaps we must look for a psychological reason,' the surgeon said thoughtfully.

Claudia nodded. 'Mr Harmon complains a good deal about noise and lack of privacy and the other patients. The routine of the ward and the proximity of people is good for some patients and bad for others, of course. It may be that Mr Harmon comes into the latter category.'

'Likes peace and quiet, does he? Well, I think we'll oblige him, Sister. I daresay he'll be complaining about that in a day or two if he's a chronic grumbler.' He smiled at her suddenly. 'But you're used to dealing with difficult patients, aren't you? I can safely leave him in your capable hands.'

'We get very few like Mr Harmon, fortunately.' But Claudia sympathised to some extent with the patient, for he seemed to bear the main brunt of Carol Gray's daily disasters. Only that morning, she'd smashed his water jug by catching it with her elbow as she reached to take his thermometer from its container above his bed. The subsequent crash had shattered more than Mr Harmon's uncertain temper!

Because he was such a bad-tempered man, he made the junior nervous and even clumsier than usual—if that was possible! Claudia was gradually becoming convinced that the girl had no future as a nurse but would make a very useful member of a demolition squad.

Trevor went away to begin the day's lengthy list of operations and Claudia set about the business of organising the transfer of the two patients, pleasing both Mr Harmon and Mr Kostapolous in the process.

She took pains to point out to the first-years that she set to the task that it simply wasn't true, as some patients declared, that a man was moved to the side ward when he was near to death. As in the case of Mr Kostapolous, many patients were returned to the main ward as soon as special nursing was no longer needed. And anyway, death on the ward was no longer commonplace now that surgery had taken such advanced strides and the general public had been alerted to having regular medical checks to catch disease in its early stages. Preventive medicine often did away with the necessity for major surgery, she explained, underlining something that they had already been told in PTS.

It was a long day of split duty for Claudia and it was after eight o'clock when she finally left the ward to go home. She was just descending the stone steps of the main entrance when she heard the sound of sirens. It was much too familiar to make her pause but she glanced with professional interest and concern at the two ambulances that travelled at speed along the High Street, blue lights flashing and sirens wailing to warn other traffic to clear their route.

Two in obvious convoy implied a bad accident, possibly on the arterial road to the coast that lay in the

hospital catchment area. It implied extra work for
Trevor, too, for he was one of the duty surgeons that
night. She'd noticed his name on the board as she passed
through Main Hall and nodded goodnight to the porter
behind the big desk.

She'd only walked a few yards when another siren and
another flashing light heralded the advent of a third
ambulance. This time, Claudia did pause and look after
the vehicle, professional instincts stirring. It looked as if
it was going to be a busy night for Accident and
Emergency and she wondered how many of the admissions would need surgery, mentally reviewing the
few available beds on Fleming.

On impulse, she hurried back to the clearing bay that
was crowded with ambulances and the intent, hurrying
figures of nurses and ambulancemen and porters. It was
obviously a major accident of some kind. Seriously
injured people were being unloaded from the ambulances, some of them with the letter M marked crudely
on their foreheads with lipstick to indicate that they'd
been given morphia by doctors at the scene of the
accident.

Knowing better than to interrupt anyone with questions, she hurried into the department to find it dealing
with the influx of casualties with its usual, unflurried
efficiency. Sister was at her desk, issuing brisk instructions to her nurses while talking on the telephone to
theatre and keeping a vigilant eye on the porters who
hurried to and from the reception area with stretcher-
trolleys and wheelchairs. More ambulances were arriving, some accompanied by police cars carrying other
injured, and a number of people were milling about to
add to the confusion.

Claudia's arrival was greeted with approval by Sister
Casualty, as she continued to be known despite the more

progressive name for her department. 'Ah, good! We can use you, Sister Hailey!' she declared directly. 'You'll know what to do without being told!'

'What's it all about, Sister?'

'A train crash. One ran into the back of another, apparently. Several dead and there are a number of serious casualties. They're bringing them to us as we're the nearest hospital with a casualty department. So far we've had ten acute surgicals and all the theatres are busy—and still they come!'

She turned back to the telephone and Claudia hurried to don a disposable apron and assist wherever she could. Doctors who'd been hastily summoned from the wards or their private quarters were making cursory examination of the injured as they arrived and directing them to be taken to theatre, X-ray or into cubicles for immediate dressing or detailed examination by colleagues.

Every pair of hands was needed. Claudia staunched bleeding and mopped up vomit and washed grime from faces and hands. She cut away blood-soaked garments, stood by during examination, gave injections and helped with stitching up deep cuts under local anaesthetic. She dealt with tears and hysteria and helped to organise the extra nurses who'd been drafted from the wards. Recognising the beginnings of cardiac arrest in a patient, she started resuscitation while waiting for the emergency team to arrive and take over. Busy and useful, observing the untiring efforts of all around her, she was proud of her profession and thankful for the training that enabled her to be of real help in assisting and comforting the victims of disaster.

She saw Eliot among the doctors who were attending to patients in the cubicles and guessed that the sound of the ambulances, together with the ever-efficient workings of the grapevine, had brought him and others hurrying to the scene. She didn't have time to speak to him and he was apparently too busy with stitching cuts and giving injections and examining bruised and broken bodies to notice her.

At first it seemed that the flow of injured would never lessen and the department also had to deal with the usual kind of casualties that kept it busy through the night in that part of London. But later arrivals from the scene of the train crash proved to be suffering from shock rather than injury and most were allowed to leave after treatment.

And then came the spate of very seriously injured patients, brought in only after hours of work by rescue teams to free them from the wreckage. But by then the pressure on all departments of the hospital had eased, the crisis was over and they could be given the very best of care . . .

CHAPTER TWELVE

IT WAS three-thirty before Claudia was free to slip away to visit her ward and find out how the night staff were coping with the emergency admissions.

Most of the surgical cases were still in theatre or intensive care but some had been moved to the wards, and Fleming had found beds for five of them. Claudia talked to the night staff nurse and then made a quick round of the ward that was her responsibility although she was officially off duty. Several of the patients were awake and restless, disturbed by the unusual bustle and the coming and going of nurses and housemen and porters. She had a few words for each of them and then made her way to the office.

Gratefully, she sipped a cup of steaming coffee and nibbled a biscuit while she talked to the staff nurse about the accident and some of the cases that had been brought in. Fifteen people had died and the number might have been much higher if the first train hadn't been slowly moving as a signal turned from red to green. Pat's hadn't been able to take all the injured but it seemed that over a hundred people had passed through A and E that night—and Pat's had maintained its long tradition of coping.

'They'll be working all night in theatre, poor devils,' Claudia said sympathetically, thinking of the backlog of cases that had been still waiting for surgery when she finally got away from A and E.

Hearing the words, recognising her distinctive voice, Trevor paused at the open office door. 'Evening, Sister!

Evening, Staff. Do I smell coffee?' He wasn't at all surprised to find an off-duty Claudia on the ward at this hour on such a night.

'Yes—and you're very welcome to a cup, Mr Page,' Claudia said promptly.

His blond hair was damp-darkened and the sickly smell of ether clung to him. His theatre greens, loose tunic and trousers, were creased and sweat-stained and he longed for a shower and a change of clothing and the chance to fall into bed and sleep. He'd finally been relieved by a fellow-surgeon after operating non-stop for nearly seven hours, cutting, clamping, repairing and sewing-up at speed, knowing that as one patient was wheeled off to recovery yet another waited in the ante-room for surgical attention. But, conscientious as ever, he hadn't felt able to go off duty until he'd done a final round of the patients admitted that night.

The staff nurse nodded in greeting and then moved towards the door. 'Excuse me—but it's time for Mr Braid's injection.' She hurried from the room, leaving sister and surgeon together.

Claudia rose to pour the coffee. 'Sit down for a few minutes, Trevor,' she said gently, discarding etiquette. 'I know that I needed a break and *I* haven't been working in theatre all these hours!'

The weary surgeon sank gratefully into a chair and ran a hand over eyes that ached from concentration and operating under hot arc lights. A nerve throbbed steadily in his cheek. 'A little bird told me that you've been working flat out in A and E,' he said. He leaned back, watching her pour the coffee with her slender, deft hands. 'I thought you were off duty and well out of it all.'

She smiled at him over her shoulder. 'I was just going home when things started happening and it was obvious that every pair of hands would count.' She handed him the cup of coffee. 'I wondered if I should be on the ward but the night staff managed perfectly well without me and I was desperately needed to help out in A and E.'

'A nasty business,' he sighed. 'Some of the casualties were in a very bad way. It was a matter of patching them up as best we could and as quickly as possible. Some of them will need a second trip to theatre in a day or two. Had a look at your quota yet, Sister?'

There was no one to overhear, all the night staff busy on the ward, but he was still being cautious, Claudia observed. 'I did a quick round. They all seem to be comfortable.' She watched him stir his coffee with the weary air of a man who found it difficult to summon up the energy to drink it. 'Trevor, you're dead on your feet!' she exclaimed in concern. 'I hope you aren't going back to theatre!'

He shook his head. 'No. Larry Thompson's taken over from me for the rest of the night. I'm going home to bed.'

'So am I,' Claudia said, stifling a yawn.

He smiled slightly. 'That sounds like an offer that even a tired man can't refuse,' he joked. Then he sobered, suddenly. 'A man needs a woman's arms about him on nights when he's haunted by reminders that he isn't immortal—and this is going to be one of those nights. I feel it in my bones . . .'

Claudia was moved by the quiet words, by the look of longing in his blue eyes. Knowing that he loved her, she wished it was possible for her to make him happy by spending what remained of the night in his arms. But it wasn't—and not only because she was still another man's wife.

Trevor was a dear, a fine man, all that she most admired and respected and she was very fond of him.

But he just didn't quicken her senses or fire her blood and she was determined that she would never again give herself to a man without wanting him as she should. She'd been given just an inkling of the delight that man and woman could bring to each other and she didn't mean to settle for less in the future. She'd cheated Eliot when she'd lain in his arms and given herself without desire. She wouldn't do that to Trevor—and she wouldn't cheat herself of the chance that one day she might experience real ecstasy and real fulfilment in the arms of a man who was right for her.

'I'll send out my thoughts to you,' she said carefully. It was a gentle rebuff. But she put a hand on his shoulder and bent to kiss his cheek, ignoring all the rules of hospital etiquette. For there was no one to see—and hadn't he earned a small token of her affection that night?

'Cold comfort!' It was disappointed. Trevor caught her fingers with a swift movement of his muscular hand. 'I want you so much, Claudia.' The touch of her hand, the warmth in her eyes and the way she'd kissed him broke through his caution and he was too tired to care if they were seen or overheard. 'I want to marry you, damn it!' he said with the sudden impatience of frustration.

'Oh, Trevor . . .' The words trailed off. She allowed her hand to lie in his clasp, slightly at a loss. He'd become so involved and she wasn't at all sure that her future lay with him!

Neither heard the soft footfall of the man who'd followed Claudia to the ward. Eliot had decided that he'd given her enough time to wonder at his apparent indifference and neglect, and paused by the open door for a few moments. Now, he turned and walked away, having seen and heard enough to convince him that she wouldn't wish to know that he cared for her all over again, and with a new kind of loving that he'd never expected to feel for any woman.

'What do you mean to do about Hailey? You can't let things drift on for ever, you know,' Trevor urged.

'These things take time,' Claudia said, rather lamely, feeling a trifle guilty because she hadn't taken even the first steps towards a divorce even though it was obvious that Eliot wouldn't oppose it and would welcome his freedom. 'It might be months before I'm free. In the meantime, I don't want you to feel tied. I mean, I'd understand if . . . I mean, if you wanted to . . . Oh, dear, I'm saying it all so badly!' She smiled at him, confused.

'Go out with other girls if I feel so inclined?' he suggested. 'That's what you mean, isn't it? Fall in love with someone else if I can manage it, because you aren't making any promises? That's really what you're saying, isn't it?'

'Something like that.' She held tightly to his hand, meeting the anxiety in his blue eyes with honesty in her own, anxious not to hurt him and trying to be fair to him. 'Everything happened in a rush. One moment we were friends and then, suddenly, you wanted to turn us into lovers with a future. I'm not really ready for that, Trevor. The last thing I want is to hurt you.'

'You're still in love with your husband,' he accused bitterly.

'*No!*' It was explosive, adamant.

He searched her face for an intent moment. 'I wonder, Claudia. I wonder if you know what you want any more.' He gently withdrew his hand and rose, almost upsetting his untouched coffee. 'Don't try to let me down lightly. It's rather too late for me not to love you.'

'I'm sorry!'

The surgeon didn't give her a chance to say more. He

walked from the room, disappointment and dismay and just a hint of anger in his expressive back. Claudia sighed. Why did life have to be so complicated all of a sudden—and all because she'd made the mistake of marrying Eliot in her salad days? She took a grain of comfort from the thought that if she'd been free she might have married Trevor—and that would have been just as much of a mistake. For neither man was right for her, after all . . .

Trevor was stiff with her at their next encounter. Claudia understood and forgave and somehow just didn't believe that they could cease to be friends all in a moment. Just now, he was hurt and disappointed and hiding behind his pride. He'd been tired and dispirited and she'd refused to give him the comfort and assurance that he needed. But he'd come round.

They'd always liked each other and they'd slipped easily into friendship—he would soon forget the momentary setback in their relationship, she felt. He'd smile in passing or they'd enjoy a moment of shared amusement at something a patient said or did during his round; or perhaps he'd arrive one day with a story about one of his patients on another ward. He'd eventually accept that her inability to love him was no bar to friendship, on and off duty—and once she was free of the marriage that bound her to Eliot, they wouldn't have to worry about grapevine gossip and hospital etiquette. In time, they might become very close, her feeling for him might change and she might respond to him in the right way, she told herself with the kind of optimism that had carried her through too many years of loving Eliot in vain.

Eliot was ignoring her existence after that very promising and heartwarming start to a new kind of relationship, she realised. It was rather puzzling that in ten days she hadn't seen hide nor hair of him. But she'd heard plenty about him from Leonie, who seemed unable to mention her work on Matthew without bringing in some quite unnecessary reference to Eliot, Claudia thought, slightly irritated.

He'd certainly charmed his way into her friend's affections. Leonie of all people ought to know just what he was and how foolish it was to trust him. But Leonie was not only seeing him almost every day on Matthew. It seemed that she'd also been meeting him almost every evening for the past week—and Claudia only discovered it by chance.

She didn't *mind*, of course. She had no reason to mind, not any more. It would be absurd for Leonie or anyone else to suppose that she was jealous of Eliot's interest in her friend and flat-mate. She was just surprised that neither had mentioned their growing involvement or their frequent meetings—and she was concerned for Leonie, who seemed to be falling in love with a totally unreliable man and wasn't prepared to heed even the smallest hint of warning.

'You said yourself how much he'd changed,' Leonie returned blithely when Claudia tried yet again, as tactfully as she knew how, to point out that Eliot was a dangerous man. He was a charmer and a flirt, he couldn't stay faithful to any woman; utterly without heart or conscience, as she knew to her cost.

'Only in some ways.' Tact didn't seem to work. She might just as well be blunt. 'Once a rake, always a rake—and I'm sure you know that he wants only one thing where you're concerned, Leonie.'

There was mischief in her friend's laughing glance. 'What makes you so sure that he hasn't had what he wants—and come back for more?'

A slight flush stained Claudia's cheeks and her mouth

tightened abruptly. 'That's between you and Eliot. Nothing to do with me.'

'You're still married to him.'

'I don't care what he does. I'm divorcing him, anyway.' The word still had an ugly sound to Claudia. Maybe that explained why she hadn't yet instructed the family solicitor to begin proceedings. 'I'm concerned for you. I don't want him to hurt you as he hurt me!'

'That won't happen,' Leonie said confidently. 'You're still judging Eliot by the way he behaved four years ago. Lots of men sow their wild oats and then settle down quite happily when they find the right woman.'

Claudia was shaken by the cool words that seemed to completely overlook the fact that Eliot had once believed *her* to be the right woman for him. Stifling resentment, she vigorously scrubbed carrots for the casserole that she was preparing for supper. 'I think you're flattered because he fancies you,' she said recklessly. 'And perhaps you think you'll be able to reform him. I know from bitter experience that it's a waste of time hoping that he'll change. He won't!'

Undismayed, Leonie reached for a newly-scrubbed baby carrot and bit into its sweet crispness. 'You couldn't do it. Maybe I can.' She looked up, smiling at Claudia with an affection and an insouciance that robbed the words of all intent to hurt. 'Don't grudge him to me, Claudia. You don't want him any more, after all.'

Claudia stifled an instinctive protest. She *did* want him—in a way that she would never admit to Leonie or anyone else. She wanted him in a way that she must suppress because it was obvious that Eliot no longer found her at all attractive and her unwelcome and newly-sparked desire for him was doomed to frustration and disappointment.

'Are you so fond of him?' It was quiet, almost

defeated. She'd never known her friend in this particular
frame of mind or this hidden-secret kind of mood and
she couldn't help wondering if Leonie was really in love
at last. If so, it was ironic that it should be Eliot who'd
been her *bête noire* for years!

'Yes, I am, very fond,' she said, unhesitatingly, with
obvious sincerity. 'How did you manage to turn him into
such an ogre without actually running him down to me or
anyone else?' she went on, marvelling. 'He really is the
nicest man!'

Claudia stiffened. 'Maybe he seems that way now! But
you never used to like him at all—and it didn't need any
word from me, good, bad or indifferent, to turn you
against him at first sight!' She felt it was a necessary
reminder as well as a defence. It was too bad of Leonie to
imply that she'd maligned Eliot in some way when she'd
always been such a loyal wife!

'Well, that's true,' Leonie conceded fairly. 'Maybe I
always knew that I'd like him too much if I once began to
like him at all. And he was your property in those days,
too. Now . . . well, things are rather different, aren't
they?'

'Very different.' A slow anger was beginning to burn
in her breast. Leonie hadn't taken Eliot away from her.
But it seemed that she had every intention of keeping
him away, just when Claudia was beginning to want him
as she'd never wanted him in earlier days. She felt a
fierce dislike of the thought of Leonie in his arms,
Leonie pleasing and delighting him, Leonie becoming
more and more important to him with the ease that had
always got her any man she wanted in the past. *She'd*
never wanted Eliot until she met him again, either—and
Claudia wished she knew what it was about him that had
suddenly swept them both off their feet with his unexpected return.

'You have your own plans for the future, don't you?' Leonie said carelessly.

'Do I?' Claudia looked at her sharply.

'Trevor Page. Going to marry him, aren't you? As soon as you're free.'

Claudia didn't remember that she'd been so forthcoming about Trevor's hopes or her own half-hearted and short-lived belief that she wished to spend the rest of her life with him. But there was obviously no other way that Leonie could have known that there'd been some talk of marriage between them.

'Plenty of time to make plans when I *am* free,' she declared. 'In the meantime, I'm perfectly happy as I am.' She chopped carrots so forcibly that one flew up in the air and landed on the floor. 'I suggest you start getting ready if you're meeting Eliot. You must have learned by now that he hates to be kept waiting.'

Leonie moved slowly towards the door. 'Do you know, sometimes I think we must be talking about two totally different men. The Eliot *I* know is nothing like the one that you describe!'

'Perhaps he underwent a frontal lobotomy when he was in Tanzania!' Claudia threw after her friend sarcastically. 'It could only have improved him—and you're welcome to the new Eliot! I still wouldn't trust him any further than I can throw him—and nor should you!'

A tinkling, untroubled laugh was her only reply. Claudia put the casserole in the oven to cook and then began to tidy the kitchen with a sudden burst of energy that she didn't immediately recognise as suppressed resentment. Resentment because Leonie was getting ready to spend a pleasant evening with a very attractive man—who happened to be *her* husband, after all—while she sat at home and fretted about the future. At the moment *that* seemed to hold only the prospect of growing older and sharper-tongued and bossier, until she eventually turned into the dragon of a ward sister that Eliot had jokingly told her she'd already become.

Heaven knew why *she* wasn't out on the town every evening with one man or another, like Leonie! Heaven knew that she had her opportunities! Heaven knew why she didn't put on a pretty frock and walk to Hoyle Street and knock on Trevor's door and throw herself into his arms—and to hell with the gossips and convention and marriage vows and Eliot and everything else! She was even more annoyed with herself for stupidly believing that Eliot wanted them to be friends and even imagining he felt a vestige of his former feeling for her, when all the time his sights had obviously been set on her pretty friend!

The following morning, Claudia was kept busy on the ward until it was time for her to attend a sisters' conference. It was presided over by Matron, as the director of nursing services continued to be known at Pat's, where old habits and long traditions found it hard to conform to new rulings.

Delegating responsibility for the ward to Julie Gordon, she made her way along to the administration wing via the stone stairways and maze of intersecting corridors that dated Pat's as a typically Victorian foundation for the care of the sick. Her route took her through out-patients with its spacious but window-less hall, crowded benches and cramped consulting-rooms.

She wasn't consciously thinking about Eliot that morning. Her mind was on the conference ahead and she wasn't aware that it was one of the days when Sir Hartley Oates held a clinic for his small patients. But she saw Eliot without surprise as she walked past the rows of necessarily patient parents and their offspring, who were waiting to see Sir Hartley or his registrar.

The children became fractious and restless at the long wait in the stuffy hall and parents became irritable through anxiety. Few nurses enjoyed working on out-patients on paediatric clinic days. Anxiety and apprehension rubbed off too easily on their own sensitivities and sickness and disability somehow seemed less acceptable when it was visited on an innocent child.

Claudia paused to study a significant cameo that caught her attention. Eliot didn't seem to notice her as he crouched to the level of a tiny boy and gently encouraged him to investigate the mysteries of a stethoscope. He obviously hoped that curiosity would overcome the child's natural fear.

It was a familiar scene for any hospital nurse who'd ever worked on a children's ward, of course. But it was Eliot's handling of the encounter and the tender interest and sympathy that illumined his lean, attractive face that tugged at her notice and even, slightly, her heart. She had never seen him at work with any of his patients before and it was an excellent opportunity to observe for herself if he was as good with children as she'd been told by Leonie and others.

The toddler's cheeks were tear-stained and the occasional sob still heaved the small breast—it seemed that it would need much more than a temporary distraction to bring a smile to a very solemn face. But the child was no longer crying and he seemed to be listening intently to Eliot's quiet voice and allowing himself to be reassured.

Fingering the rubber tubing of the stethoscope, the small boy gazed at the white-coated stranger with wide eyes that held the dawn of trust and the merest beginnings of a smile. Eliot's hand moved from the thin shoulder to cradle the tousled head in an involuntary and entirely natural gesture of genuine caring and infinite tenderness. It caught unexpectedly at Claudia's heart.

The child tensed, still not sure. Then, suddenly, he relaxed. Sliding his hand into Eliot's, he nodded his willingness to accompany him into the consulting-room.

Eliot straightened and looked directly into Claudia's eyes. For a moment, they were locked in mutual understanding and satisfaction with the profession that was always demanding but offered its own rewards in so many ways.

It was a moment of communion such as she'd never expected to share with him, transcending the highs and lows of their personal and very troubled relationship. It was a moment when Claudia realised with sudden clarity that in all the years of loving, she'd never really known Eliot—or liked him quite so much.

She smiled at him. Something burned in the depths of those dark eyes that she didn't recognise and didn't have time to analyse. Abruptly, that strange and unfamiliar glow faded. Then he nodded to her, unsmiling and impersonal, and turned away with the toddler clinging to his hand and tugging to regain his attention.

Claudia hurried on to the conference, her heart thudding in very strange fashion . . .

CHAPTER THIRTEEN

FOR NEARLY an hour, Claudia listened and made notes, asked and answered questions, and hoped that she gave a convincing performance as a cool, composed and dedicated ward sister. But she didn't feel at all cool or composed and her dedication to nursing suddenly seemed to have become secondary to other needs in her life.

She kept remembering the way that Eliot had looked at a frail little boy, the way that he'd put his hand, with tenderness, to a small blond head and the way her foolish heart had jolted when he glanced up and met her gaze with that oddly disturbing glow in the depths of his dark eyes.

For once, there'd been no hint of mockery or light-hearted challenge in the way he'd looked at her. She'd felt an involuntary response to a core of sensitivity and integrity and compassion that she'd never known or even suspected in earlier days. She'd felt liking, admiration, respect for him as a doctor—and something more. *Love* for the man! Not just renewed and restored but totally different—and with no chance at all of being returned, for he'd long since ceased to care anything for her, Claudia realised with a sinking of her heart.

Leaving Matron's office when the conference was finished, she could have returned to the ward by a different route. She didn't. She crossed the still-busy out-patients department just as Eliot emerged from a consulting-room with a young mother who held a baby in her arms. The girl was on the verge of tears. The infant was a pathetic little scrap of humanity. Eliot was kindly, reassuring. Then a nurse ushered mother and child away and he turned to notice Claudia who'd paused to speak as soon as opportunity offered.

She smiled at him, warm and friendly, encouraging. 'You seem to have your hands full this morning.'

He ignored the light words. 'Slightly off course, aren't you, Sister?'

Claudia looked in vain for a vestige of a smile in his eyes or voice. There was a grimness about the mobile mouth and a hardness in his expression that was dismaying. She told herself that he was being discreet. The cool tone and the formal address were for the benefit of watching eyes and listening ears, of course.

'I've just come from Matron's office. It's a short cut,' she explained.

He raised an eyebrow. 'Summoned to the presence? I thought you left naughty goings-on to your nurses.'

'Sisters' conference.' She wondered if he could hear the heavy thump of her heart and if the force of her renewed feelings were creating a kind of tension between them or if it was just foolish fancy.

He nodded. 'Of course. Absurd of me to suppose that you could do anything wrong or make any mistakes,' he said cuttingly. 'After all, you're a paragon of virtue—the soul of efficiency and a credit to the nursing profession. All starch and no heart.'

Her smile felt pinned to her lips. The sneering words were so obviously meant to hurt. She swallowed pain as well as pride and pretended to believe that he was teasing her. 'A pearl beyond price,' she agreed. 'How are you, anyway? I haven't seen you in days. How is everything?'

'Everything is fine. Isn't Leonie keeping you up to date?'

Somehow, she managed a light laugh. 'Oh, I haven't seen much of Leonie, either. It's like Box and Cox these days . . . I go in as she comes out, and vice versa!' She hesitated and then went on as though they were the best of friends. 'I owe you a meal, by the way. Why don't you come to supper this evening and we'll catch up on each other's news?' It was blatant but she didn't care.

Eliot looked at her with hard eyes. 'I think we must both have better things to do,' he said, cool and curt. He nodded to the hovering and slightly curious staff nurse who'd dutifully kept her distance while doctor and sister were talking. 'I'll have my next patient in now, please, Nurse.'

Claudia, dismissed, felt the rebuff like a blow. She hurried away, her heart feeling as though it was squeezed by a brutal hand. He'd hurt her before, so many times. But this was a new and devastating kind of hurt. Before, he'd wounded her with selfish, unthinking behaviour and a forgivable inability to love as deeply as she did. He'd never been deliberately cruel, setting out to wound, watching for the effect and noting it with a kind of satisfaction.

She knew that nothing could remain of the love that Eliot had once felt for her, of course. But she'd foolishly hoped that something might have emerged from the ashes. A little liking or some degree of affection or, at the very least, a professional respect for all that she'd achieved in her nursing career. But the way he'd looked, the way he'd spoken and turned away, implied that he thought of her with dislike and a contempt that wasn't even tempered with his usual mocking amusement.

It was such a sudden and unexpected change of attitude that Claudia could only wonder what she'd said or done to alienate him. Or perhaps he was regretting the sentiment that had led him to be nice to her in his first weeks at Pat's and now he wished her to know that he had lost all interest.

She'd begun to believe that they could be friends, despite everything. She'd begun to warm to him all over again and she'd found herself wanting him in a new and very disturbing fashion that was too ready to overlook the past and give little thought to the future. In fact, she'd come dangerously near to making a fool of herself a second time, she realised—and all for a man who just wasn't worth the high cost of loving him!

That brief encounter shadowed the rest of the day for Claudia. Hurt and dismayed far more than she meant to admit, she didn't feel her usual glow of satisfaction as she surveyed the ward and her patients and saw to it that her team of nurses were doing their work cheerfully and well. She almost wondered why she'd worked so hard and longed so much to be a ward sister when at heart she wanted more from life than nursing offered, rewarding and worthwhile though it could be as a career. She almost felt that she could bid goodbye to Fleming and Pat's and even nursing without a twinge of regret if happiness ever beckoned.

Unaccountably, without rhyme or reason, it seemed that her dream of real happiness was still linked with Eliot—and, therefore, forever out of reach.

One result of her topsy-turvy emotions was a complete loss of patience with the first-year that everyone laughingly knew as Calamity Jane. There had been some slight improvement in the girl's work and behaviour due to Claudia's patience, sympathetic handling and firm but kindly pep-talks. But disaster had been stalking the pretty Carol Gray for days—and it overtook her at last, just when Claudia was in no mood to be tolerant or sympathetic or understanding.

During the course of that day, the junior flooded one

of the bathrooms, lost a patient's folder *en route* to X-Ray, gave a patient on a fat-free diet the wrong lunch, dropped a tray of sterilised instruments as she took them from the autoclave and finally managed to collide with Claudia when she was hurrying along the ward with a newly-mixed feed that was destined for the intragastric tube of a post-op patient. Most of the contents of the container survived the impact, but some splashed Claudia's dark blue frock and the girl's apron.

It was a minor incident compared to some in recent weeks. But it was the last straw for Claudia, who suddenly lost her temper with the exasperating girl who'd been a thorn in her side since her first day on Fleming.

'You stupid girl!' she flared, eyes blazing. 'You really are impossible—a danger to yourself and to everyone else! I'm suspending you from duty. Leave the ward immediately and report to Matron tomorrow morning. I am not going to put up with your disrupting presence on my ward for one more day!'

The girl was flushed, angry in her turn. The incident had taken place in full view of a curious ward. The patients were staring, listening hard. The nurses had stopped what they were doing to observe the unprecedented scene between ward sister and the first-year nurse and there was sympathy for both parties.

'It was an accident, Sister!' Carol declared defensively. 'You can't send me off duty for an accident!'

Claudia froze. 'Don't argue with me, Nurse,' she said sternly. 'Just do as you're told.'

The junior stood her ground, defiant. 'I can never do anything right for you, Sister. But this time it was as much your fault as mine. *You* weren't looking, either! It isn't fair to report me—and I don't believe you have the right to suspend me just like that!'

Claudia's eyes and voice were icy. 'You seem to be challenging my authority, Nurse Gray.'

'That's right. I am!' No longer so sure of herself in the face of Claudia's coolness, it sounded like bravado.

'Then I suggest that you repeat your words in front of Matron.' She looked round for Julie Gordon and beckoned to her. The staff nurse hurried to join the obviously angry sister and the rather pale junior. 'Take charge of the ward, please, Staff. I won't be long. Come with me, Nurse Gray.' It was brisk, peremptory.

Carol Gray hesitated, looking to the staff nurse for support. It wasn't forthcoming although there was a hint of sympathy in Julie's eyes. Everyone knew that Sister Hailey wasn't her usual sunny self, even if no one knew the cause—and it had seemed inevitable that the scatter-brained but popular junior would bear the brunt of her displeasure before the day was out.

Reluctantly, the first-year trailed in Claudia's wake, her initial defiance fading rapidly before growing dismay as she realised that she could lose the job that she was learning to love. 'I'm sorry, Sister,' she blurted as soon as the ward doors had swung shut behind them. 'I didn't mean to answer back . . .' It was the worst crime in the book for a junior nurse, and she knew it.

Claudia looked at her coldly. 'But you did—and on the ward, of all places! In front of patients! I don't know what they thought of such behaviour but I know what I think of it, Nurse. You've shown yourself to be thought-less and irresponsible and totally unsuited to a nursing career!'

'Yes, Sister. I'm sorry, Sister.' She looked down at the floor to hide the brimming tears.

It might have been automatic response. It sounded like genuine contrition but Claudia wasn't in the mood to relent. She was much too angry. That *her* ward should be the setting for such a scene and *her* patients subjected to such behaviour from one of *her* nurses was quite unforgivable. She prided herself on the smooth running of the ward for which she was responsible—and she was furious that the incident would soon be recounted in every corner of Pat's and be greatly exaggerated in the telling. She didn't doubt that the junior would be represented as the innocent victim while she appeared as the harsh and unfeeling villain. It was the price that one apparently paid for having reached the exalted and often lonely position of ward sister, she thought sadly.

'I'm extremely disappointed, Nurse Gray. I was just beginning to feel that you might make a nurse, after all—and I believe you've been trying to make up for a very bad start. But you went completely to pieces today and there's no place on my ward for an incompetent junior. Nor will I tolerate the way you spoke to me and I'm sure that Matron will agree to my request for you to be transferred to another ward.'

'Please don't do that, Sister! It will be such a black mark against me—and I *like* working on Fleming! I really am sorry that I was rude and it won't happen again—and I will try harder, I promise.'

'I've no faith in your promises,' Claudia told her coldly. 'I've heard too many of them. You've consistently let me down and I'm not giving you any more chances.' As she spoke, the thought of Eliot flashed into her mind. It was exactly how she felt about him—and it seemed that her pain and disappointment and deeply-felt anger with herself for being so ready to love and trust all over again was venting its force on the youthful junior.

Carol Gray shrugged, defeated. 'You're so hard,' she said, accusingly. 'Don't you remember what it was like when you were a first-year? I don't think I want to be a nurse if it means that I shall end up a sour old maid like you!'

Tempted to slap the pretty and suddenly defiant face, Claudia laughed instead. It was an angry laugh, without a trace of humour. 'I don't think there's any danger that *you'll* suffer such a fate! But you have your facts wrong, you know. I may be hard and sour but I'm not an old maid! I was married when I was a scatter-brained first-year like you!'

It was impulsive and instantly regretted as she saw the surprise and swift calculation in the girl's eyes. Eliot wouldn't be pleased, either, she thought, knowing that her words would be repeated at the earliest opportunity.

'Were, you, Sister? I didn't know that!' The first-year hesitated. 'I didn't mean to be rude but I don't want to be dragged off to Matron's office like a naughty child. Put me on Report if you must—and I'll go off duty right now if you insist. But I shall maintain that it was an accident and that you were unfair—and I shall tell Matron that you've had a down on me ever since I came to work on this ward.'

'That isn't true!' Claudia said quickly. But even as she refuted the accusation, she had a sudden and vivid recollection of Julie saying the same thing on one occasion. Was it possible that she had always been a little jealous of the pretty and popular junior who seemed to sail through life with such ease and could shrug off any setback with a smile? Was it possible that she'd always disapproved of the girl's light-hearted, irresponsible attitude to life that reminded her so much of Eliot? Was it possible that she'd used Carol Gray as a scapegoat for all the irritation and frustration that Eliot had evoked in her since his return? A return that had virtually coincided with the girl's first day on Fleming as her newest junior nurse, she recalled suddenly.

'You've never liked me, Sister, and you've watched me like a hawk waiting to pounce on every mistake I make! It isn't surprising that I haven't done at all well on Fleming!' Carol added defensively.

Claudia studied her for a long moment, torn between professional outrage and a reluctant sympathy for a first-year who might have suffered at her hands in the past few weeks. 'Very well, Nurse. I won't take you to Matron today. I think you need time to cool down. But I do want you to leave the ward. If you really feel that I haven't been fair to you then perhaps you will do better on another ward with a different sister in charge of your training,' she said firmly.

'Yes, Sister. Thank you, Sister.' She turned away, more disappointed than rebellious. Then she paused, turned back. 'Are you married to the new registrar, Sister? Eliot Hailey? Is *he* your husband?'

Claudia was incapable of an outright lie. 'That's right. Now run along, Nurse Gray. I must get back to the ward!'

'Someone said you were cousins!'

'Someone made a mistake,' she returned coolly and pushed her way through the swing-doors before the girl could hurl any more questions at her head.

It was almost a relief to have it out in the open, she admitted. It was really rather absurd that she'd gone to such lengths to keep her marriage a secret for so long. Now, there would probably be a great deal more talk than if everyone had known from the beginning, she thought ruefully.

Later, writing her report for Matron, her hand hesitated and hovered above the page when it came to detailing the first-year's crime. She was tempted to let the girl off one more time. But she knew that it was out of the question. Her authority had been challenged and she simply couldn't let it pass. Carol Gray might be grateful but she would also preen herself on having got away with a serious breach of hospital etiquette—and she would cease to have any respect for her, Claudia knew. It was obviously true that she would do better on a different ward, anyway. No matter what the reason, Claudia just didn't have the patience she ought to have where the girl was concerned. So she put the junior's name on Report and added a request to be present at the inevitable interview.

Leonie was out that evening when she arrived home at the end of a long and dispiriting day. Out with Eliot, no doubt . . . Claudia tossed her cloak on a chair and went to make some tea for herself. The telephone rang while she was filling the kettle and she flew to answer it as if she was nineteen again and waiting on a call from the man she loved!

It wasn't Eliot. Taking the message for Leonie from yet another of her boyfriends, she wondered what kind of fool she was to have hoped, even for a moment, that it might be him. Her heart was heavy as she realised just how much of a fool she actually was.

Loving Eliot was forgivable folly . . . *once*! To love him again, and so much more deeply, when she knew the inevitable outcome was totally unforgivable stupidity, Claudia told herself wearily.

This was a new kind of loving to anything she'd known in the past. Then, she'd loved him with a girl's blind, unthinking devotion that had wanted to make a god out of a very human man. No wonder he'd scrambled so hastily from that uncomfortable pedestal! Now, she loved like a woman—and, as a woman, she felt an all-consuming ache of desire and despair for the happiness they might have known if only he'd tried to win back her love and convince her that their destiny lay together.

But he hadn't. For he didn't love her or want her any more and he didn't feel, as she did, that their lives were irrevocably linked by a youthful, impulsive marriage. He wanted to be free.

She was still up, watching a late-night weepie entirely in keeping with her mood, when Leonie came home. Claudia surreptitiously flicked away the tears that were threatening to spill and was ready with a bright smile for her friend and flat-mate.

'Nice evening?' She rose and switched off the television. 'You're early, aren't you? By *your* standards,' she added lightly, teasingly.

'Eliot wasn't feeling well.' Leonie dropped the words carelessly but she watched and waited for Claudia's reaction.

It was confirmation that they'd spent yet another evening together, just as she'd suspected. With an effort, Claudia swallowed the unexpectedly bitter pill that he preferred Leonie's company to her own these days. No doubt Leonie was more amusing, more admiring and much more responsive to his amorous overtures than she'd allowed herself to be!

'I hope you did the ministering angel bit like a good Pat's nurse. Put him to bed, took his pulse, soothed the fevered brow . . .' It was blithe, apparently indifferent, as she moved about the room, plumping cushions, putting away books and papers, leaving everything neat for the night.

'You know perfectly well that doctors are the worst patients in the world,' Leonie protested. 'I tried to fuss but he wasn't having any. He wouldn't even admit to feeling ill but he's obviously running a temperature and he doesn't look at all well. So I said I wanted an early night. He still insisted on bringing me home. I only hope he's gone straight back to bed with a couple of aspirin.'

'You should have brought him in for a hot drink.'

'I suggested it. He didn't want to disturb you.'

'Thoughtful of him!' He hadn't wanted to run the risk of seeing her, in truth, she thought heavily. Hadn't he shown her earlier in the day that he had nothing to say to her? She yawned, stretched, moved towards her room. 'Well, I'm off to my own bed. What seems to be wrong with Eliot, anyway?' It sounded like an afterthought, just as she'd intended.

'Oh, a touch of summer flu, I should think. Probably nothing to worry about.' Leonie said reassuringly.

'So who's worried?'

Leonie followed her into the bedroom, looking her surprise. 'Whatever happened to the conscientious Sister Hailey?'

Claudia shrugged. 'Off duty—and Eliot isn't my patient or my concern. Surely you don't expect me to rush round to his flat clutching a thermometer and a packet of aspirins!'

'No. I just thought you might take a little interest in his welfare.'

'Not any more,' she said firmly.

Leonie sat on the bed and looked at the pale and lovely face reflected in the dressing-table mirror as Claudia loosened her long hair and ran a brush through the gleaming waves and rich curls. 'I suppose you know that he was very ill just before he came back to England?'

'Yes. He obviously wasn't quite fit when he started the new job and I daresay he's been overdoing things and lowered his resistance to infection.' It was carefully matter of fact. 'It's only a mild bug that's going the rounds. He'll live.'

'You've changed so much since you took charge of Fleming,' Leonie marvelled, without admiration. 'I never thought that you could be so hard, so unfeeling—about anyone, let alone Eliot!'

Claudia spun on the stool, glowering. 'Reproaching me? That's rich! You've been telling me for years to stop caring about Eliot. Suddenly he isn't too well and you think I ought to act the loving, anxious wife! Very consistent! Anyway, he doesn't need me while he has you to worry about him and I'm the last person he'd want fussing round him. Haven't you noticed that I don't exist for him any more!'

'No. But it seems that *you* have,' Leonie said quietly, with meaning.

'And that's just the way I want it.' Claudia drew off the silk kimono, flung it across a chair and slipped between the sheets. 'It's late, Leonie—and I don't want to spend half the night talking about Eliot. I shan't lose any sleep because he's caught cold, either!'

She burrowed into the pillows so pointedly that Leonie rose and went from the room with a murmured goodnight, switching off the light as she went.

Claudia lay still and tense, staring at the patch of light that fell across the sitting-room from Leonie's bedroom until it eventually vanished and she was left staring into the darkness.

It was foolish to worry about Eliot just because Leonie thought he was running a temperature and didn't look well. There was probably nothing wrong but a slight cold—it had made more of an impact because he wasn't as fit as he should be after that attack of fever. There was really no reason to suppose that he'd gone down with a recurrence of the same fever that had laid him low in Tanzania, she told herself firmly.

But she didn't sleep very well that night . . .

CHAPTER FOURTEEN

ELIOT didn't turn up for work the next day. Or the following day. The grapevine reported that he was ill and Claudia was anxious. But Leonie didn't seem unduly worried. There was a mild viral infection going the rounds and he'd probably picked it up, she declared lightly. No doubt he'd sensibly taken to his bed for a few days. As he wasn't answering his telephone he obviously wanted to be left alone.

Claudia decided to call at the flat, anyway. She was off duty that afternoon and it seemed the least she could do to show some interest in his welfare and ask if he needed anything. Being ill was a miserable business when one lived alone, after all—and few men bothered to make proper meals for themselves when they were well.

There was no reason why Leonie should concern herself about him, of course. *She* wasn't his wife! They might be on the verge of divorce but Claudia wanted to see him, to do what she could for him, to show that she still cared what happened to him. Maybe she was all kinds of a fool but she couldn't bear to think of him alone and sick, with no one to alleviate some of the miseries of discomfort and depression that usually accompanied the flu.

She hurried round to Hoyle Street as soon as she was free to leave the ward in Lesley Wilmot's capable hands. Concerned for Eliot, she almost didn't care what happened to her patients or if her team of nurses could cope in her absence.

Her steps slowed as she neared the house. Impulse

had carried her so far but now she was unsure of her reception. For Eliot didn't seem to like her very much these days and he might think her a poor substitute for Leonie. He might not even open the door to her, she thought nervously.

One problem was solved just as she reached the house. Someone she knew happened to be coming out and he obligingly held the front door open so that she could enter without having to announce herself and ask for admission over the outside intercom. She nodded and smiled, thanking him. She'd known Paul Saunders in her third year when he was a houseman. Now he was a gynae registrar and it seemed that he was one of Eliot's neighbours. She wondered if they knew each other but he was gone before she could ask him.

She was glad to have been spared a probable rebuff on the doorstep. With a fast-beating heart, she mounted the narrow stairs to the top of the house and rang the bell of Eliot's flat. Waiting, she recalled the day when he'd brought her to see it as though he was a prospective tenant and had then coolly announced that he'd already moved in. She'd been so annoyed with him. That had been her first and only visit, but she knew that Leonie was a frequent and obviously welcome visitor. She tried not to think about her friend's involvement with Eliot as she rang again.

It seemed a disturbingly long time before the door was finally opened in answer to a third peal at the bell. Eliot was wearing nothing but a hastily-donned towelling robe and a day's growth of beard. His hair was tousled. Claudia observed the pallor beneath his tan and the smudges that underlined the deep-set dark eyes and her heart turned over in her breast.

He scowled down at her. 'I can do without *you*,' he said bluntly.

'Yes, I know.' Claudia brushed past him, determined that he shouldn't turn her away. 'But I expect you need *someone*.'

'Not *you*. I don't need you or your sympathy or your misguided sense of duty. You don't owe me anything,' he told her brusquely. But he closed the door of the flat.

Longing to put her arms about him and draw his dark head to the breast that ached with love for him, Claudia contented herself with reaching for his wrist and feeling for the pulse in professional manner. Eliot wrenched his hand away with an angry exclamation. Undeterred, she put the back of her hand to his brow, his cheek. He was burning. He moved away from her touch, resentfully, glowering.

'You ought to be in bed,' she said briskly, rather more anxious about him than she wanted him to know.

'I was in bed, damn you!' He drew the robe more tightly about his lean frame, tightened the cord with hands that shook slightly. 'What the hell are you doing here, Claudia? I don't need a nurse and I don't want you around to make me feel worse than I already do! Just go away—and take your bloody bedside manner with you!'

Claudia refused to feel hurt. She hadn't expected a welcome, after all. 'I wanted to know how you were.'

'I'm fine.'

'Oh, Eliot! You're obviously ill,' she said, impatient with concern.

His mouth tightened. 'I don't need anything that you can do for me. What do you know about tropical fever? It's only a mild attack and I know how to treat it. I still have some quinine that I brought back with me and it's doing the trick. Satisfied?'

'When did you last have something to eat?'

He sighed. 'I don't know. This morning—yesterday. I can't remember. I haven't felt like eating.'

'Well, I don't suppose it's done you any harm as long as you've had plenty to drink. Have you a thermometer? I want to take your temperature.'

He gave a short, sharp laugh. 'For God's sake, Claudia. Get back to your ward and play the nurse to your heart's content and leave me alone, there's a good girl. I can take care of myself.'

'Eliot, I'm staying. You're far from well and I want to look after you,' she said quietly, without pride.

'The Florence Nightingale touch!' he mocked. 'You just can't forget that you're a nurse, can you?'

'I'm not here as a nurse. I'm here as your wife.'

'It's rather late in the day to decide that your place is by my side, isn't it?'

She looked at him quickly, surprised by the touch of bitterness that underlay the words. 'I never wanted to be anywhere else, Eliot,' she reminded him.

A little anger began to throb in the pulse of his jaw. 'That isn't the way I remember it. You never wanted to be anywhere but on a ward surrounded by grateful patients who didn't make unwelcome demands on you! You were so involved with nursing that you never had enough time for me or the slightest interest in my needs. As it was in the beginning, is now and ever shall be . . .' His voice shook. So did his tall frame with the sudden force of his feelings as four years of disappointment and dismay and despair swept over him all over again.

The way he trembled and the wild way he spoke made Claudia wonder if he was delirious. Concerned, she went to him and put an arm about him. 'Eliot, I didn't come to quarrel with you,' she said, contrite. 'Or to rake over the past. It's the present that should concern us both—and right now I want to get you into bed.'

He looked down at her, mouth twisting with ironic

humour. 'This is so sudden,' he mocked. 'Warm and willing at last! Who do I thank for the thaw? Page, presumably . . .'

Claudia allowed the words to pass. 'Please, Eliot. You really should be in bed and you aren't doing yourself any good by being so stubborn.'

'I can put myself to bed, thanks, Sister! I'm not one of your patients.' He thrust her away angrily. 'You might run a ward to your own and everyone else's satisfaction. You aren't running my life—not any more!'

'As if I ever did!' she returned with sudden spirit. 'You always went your own way without a thought for me or anyone else!'

'Then we are two of a kind, my love,' he drawled, dark eyes glittering. 'We seem to be well-suited in every way but one.'

A slight warmth rushed into her face. The mocking, meaningless endearment hurt her. So did the dry reminder of the frigidity that had clouded their married life and slowly but surely destroyed it. But if that was all that stood between them and eventual happiness then there was surely new hope for the future!

'Some things *do* change, Eliot,' she said, wondering if he'd remember a remark he'd made in this flat, finding it terribly hard to put into words the change he'd wrought in her on that very day.

His eyes narrowed abruptly. His memory was as good as her own. He searched her face intently. 'I'd like to believe you.'

She smiled. 'I find it hard to believe, too. But you're a very attractive man,' she said, making light of it. 'Why shouldn't I want you?' Desperately she hoped that he would realise that the levity was a cloak for the intensity of her feelings. Didn't he use it himself often enough— and for the very same reason?

He shook his head, doubtful. 'That isn't why you're here, Claudia.'

She swallowed. 'It's part of it.'

'What's the rest of it?'

'The rest has always been the same. I've always loved you,' she said quietly.

He stiffened. Suddenly he turned and walked into the bedroom as if she'd said the last thing that he wanted to hear. Claudia's heart plummeted. But she followed him into the room that had its curtains drawn against the bright sunshine of the summer afternoon. There was enough light to show her the state of the place, however. A trail of discarded clothing across the floor, the tangled sheets and bunched pillows, the confusion of the cluttered bedside table and the telephone wire that he'd jerked from the jack against interruption of the sleep he desperately needed.

Claudia stopped short. 'Heavens! Who dropped the bomb!'

'I think you just did.' Eliot turned to look at her, unsmiling. He'd walked away so that he could marshal his emotions and muster his thoughts, but she hadn't given him the time he needed. His head and heart were throbbing and he still didn't know what to believe—or what to say or do.

It didn't sound as though he was pleased, Claudia thought heavily. But why should he be? He'd stopped loving her long ago. He'd been glad to believe that she'd ceased to love him.

'Did you mean any of it, Claudia?' he demanded abruptly.

'All of it,' she said firmly.

'You've been giving a very good performance of indifference in the last few weeks.'

'I lost my way for a while,' she said frankly. 'I really

thought you didn't matter any more.' She began to pick up things from the floor, needing to be occupied, not wishing to meet the eyes that couldn't hold any of the things she wanted to read in them. 'Eliot, let's not talk about it any more just now. You really aren't well enough. Please get into bed!'

'Just as you say, Sister.' He threw off his robe.

'Just a minute, I'd better straighten it first,' she said hastily. Though she was his wife as well as a trained nurse, she was nevertheless suddenly shy of his tall, lean body, bronzed almost all over by the African sun.

He ran his hands through his hair as she glanced at him. The muscles rippled in his back and chest and strong shoulders. He was magnificently masculine and she was abruptly aware of his potent sexuality and the physical need that he'd awakened in her too late.

Carefully not looking at him again, she began to straighten sheets and plump pillows as though her life depended on it, much too conscious of him, fighting the urge to turn into his arms and raise her face to be kissed and beg him to love and need her as she loved and needed him. With heart and soul and eager body, for ever and always. For the rest of her life.

Watching her as she busied herself with sheets and pillows, Eliot's eyes rested on the tiny waist and trim hips, the tautness of small breasts straining against the thin material of her uniform frock as she reached across the bed. He was moved and enchanted by the shyness in the way she kept her face averted from him. He dearly wanted to believe that she still loved him. He loved her very much.

Her unexpected arrival that afternoon seemed an answer to the prayer of longing that had filled his mind and heart while he battled with the attack of tropical fever. But the depressing conviction that he'd never win back his wife for all the wanting, that he'd lost the only woman he'd ever really loved and had only himself to blame, had overwhelmed him.

Pride had kept him from welcoming her with any warmth. Pride had kept him from admitting his need for the love she was offering. But pride couldn't keep him from admiring and aching and yearning—and, inevitably for a sensual and ardent man, his body stirred with the desire that her loveliness evoked. He wanted to reach out for her, take her into his arms, but he hesitated, remembering the coldness that he hadn't been able to overcome in those early days. He didn't think he could bear to be rebuffed or disappointed—not now, when love and need were both so much greater than before.

'There! That should be more comfortable,' Claudia declared, resorting to the bright, impersonal tone of the trained nurse to conceal the disturbance of her emotions. 'Get into bed and I'll see if I can find something to tempt your appetite.'

He looked at her with a smile in the dark eyes. 'There's really only one thing that I fancy,' he said softly.

Her own smile wavered before the glow that seemed to set her tingling. 'Well . . . ?' she said, suddenly breathless.

'I want you.'

Her heart shook and her body melted. Before she could smile, shake her head, return a light and defensive reply, he put his hands to her head and drew out the pins that kept her hair in its neat coil. The rich mass fell about her shoulders and framed her face.

Claudia looked up at him, startled and unsure. It was impossible to mistake his meaning, the desire that was in his look, his touch, the tension of his body. Loving him, wanting him, eager to give for his delight as well as her own, she hesitated. He hadn't said one word of love, she thought sadly—and she wanted so much for him to love as she did, to want her as his wife once more in every way, to offer her a second chance of real and lasting happiness.

'I want you,' he said again, husky with longing. He cradled her face in his hands and looked deep into the beautiful amber eyes. 'More than anything in the world.'

He touched her lips with his own, light, tentative, seeking. Claudia couldn't speak or move for the wave of emotion that flooded through her entire being, a tidal wave of love and longing and intense desire. His hands slid down to her shoulders and gripped so hard that they bruised while he kissed her, very gently, urging her to response.

His kiss became deeper, more sensual, and her lips slowly warmed and parted and she sensed rather than heard his soft sigh of satisfaction. A hand moved to twine in her long hair and cradle her head, holding it firmly so that she couldn't escape the growing intensity of passion in the way he kissed her. Her heart was beating so hard and so high in her throat that she could scarcely breathe. His free hand was busy with the buttons of her dark blue frock and soon the long fingers slid across her breast in caressing exploration.

Claudia began to tremble as her body quickened to the intimacy of his touch as it had never done in the past. Eliot held her very close, straining her against him as though he would never let her go again, and the fierce throb of his body's need sent desire dancing through her like a flame.

'Eliot . . .' It was low, half-hearted protest, prompted by the need to be loved as much as desired—and a murmur of warning as she suddenly remembered that his body burned as much from the forgotten fever as the kindled passion. He let go, so abruptly and so angrily that she staggered and clutched at him for support. 'Oh, hold me!' she cried with a desperation born of need. She reached for him, urgent with love and longing, terrified of losing him all over again.

He gripped her hands, holding her away from him with a challenge in the dark eyes. 'Make up your mind, for God's sake! I don't know what you want! Tell me!' he cried fiercely. For answer, Claudia drew his hands to her breasts in a simple gesture that told him all he needed to know.

He caught her to him in sudden delight. '*Oh, my love,*' he said, low and tenderly and with never a hint of the mockery that had tinged the endearment in previous days.

He enfolded her in a loving embrace and Claudia slid her arms about his neck and kissed him, giving herself gladly to the heat of passion that finally melted every last vestige of the ice that had frozen his love rather than killed it completely.

Carried away by the flooding desire and the longing for a new beginning to the marriage that they'd entered into so hopefully, Claudia forgot everything but the sensual delight of his kiss, the exciting caress of his hands on her body, the tempestuous urgency in the way that he took her down to the waiting bed . . .

It was enchantment such as she'd never known or ever expected to know, sensual and soaring and utterly satisfying. Magic moments to remember for a lifetime and enhanced by the conviction that there was a great deal of love as well as the molten flame of passion in his powerful and competent lovemaking. Claudia held her husband close, with love, lips pressed to his bare, bronzed shoulder while he lay with his head on her breast, a touch of tenderness in the slow caress of his hand across her face and hair.

For a few minutes they were both still and silent, closer than they'd ever been, afraid to break the spell of a new and very precious intimacy. Then a rivulet of sweat began to trickle down his bare back, irritating him beyond endurance in that mood of heightened sensitivity.

He shifted his position slightly. Claudia clung, unwilling to lose a moment that might never come again, a moment when love had bound them so closely. Love that had somehow survived despite selfishness and misunderstanding and long separation.

'Let me go, darling,' he said gently, with a quick kiss. Reluctantly she released him and he reached for his robe and shrugged into it. His hair was clinging damply to his brow and sweat streaked his tanned and handsome face.

Claudia put a loving hand to brush a strand of dark hair from his eyes, smiling at him. Then her hand moved to stroke his lean cheek in loving caress—and instantly she realised that the heat had gone from his skin.

'You're a lot cooler!' she exclaimed, thankfully. 'I'm sure your temperature's gone down!'

'I'm sure my blood pressure's sky-high,' he teased, eyes dancing. He captured her fingers and took them to his lips. 'But I'm certainly feeling much better. Your brand of medicine seems to have worked wonders, Sister Hailey.'

'I don't think Matron would approve!'

'Nor will I if you go around giving it to anyone else,' he warned. 'I've waited too long and wanted you too much to share you!'

'There isn't anyone but you, Eliot. There never has been and there never will be,' she said with truth.

He put his arms about her and held her in a gentle and

very tender embrace. 'I haven't been a good husband, Claudia, any more than you've been a good wife. I think we deserve each other. Stay with me.'

It was so typically Eliot that she felt a spark of indignation that was instantly quenched as she realised the love and longing and need in his quiet tone, in his dark eyes, in the way he held her.

Still she hesitated, searching his handsome face with doubtful eyes. Could she really trust this prodigal husband who'd wasted four years of their lives as well as the first and precious chance of happiness? Could she really trust him when he promised a happy ending to a new and better beginning? Could she really be the wife that he wanted?

They'd failed each other so badly in those early days. There'd been so many faults on both sides, she finally admitted. But at least they could look back and realise their mistakes and determine to avoid them in the future.

They were both different people these days. Older, wiser, knowing what they really wanted, willing to work at creating and keeping their happiness. They had much to give each other, Claudia felt—and how could she be happy without him, when even the nursing she loved couldn't give her the fulfilment and satisfaction and rewards of marriage.

'Can I make you happy, Eliot?' she asked quietly. 'I love you but I don't know if that's enough . . . not any more.' His happiness was so much more important than her own or anything else, she realised, knowing that the quality of her love for him had changed for the better in more ways than one.

'Oh, Claudia . . .' Her name was a murmur of loving endearment. He touched his lips to her hair, his arms tightening about her. 'We can only try to make each other happy, to fulfil each other's needs, to love each other more with every year. That's what marriage is all about—and it's time we tried it like people who really care about each other's happiness. Will you?'

'I will,' she said softly, turning it into a vow that she made once more and with the conviction that this time there would be no regret, no heartache or humiliation.

Only a shared and lasting love.

Mills & Boon

4 Doctor Nurse Romances
FREE

Coping with the daily tragedies and ordeals of a busy hospital, and sharing the satisfaction of a difficult job well done, people find themselves unexpectedly drawn together. Mills & Boon Doctor Nurse Romances capture perfectly the excitement, the intrigue and the emotions of modern medicine, that so often lead to overwhelming and blissful love. By becoming a regular reader of Mills & Boon Doctor Nurse Romances you can enjoy EIGHT superb new titles every two months plus a whole range of special benefits: your very own personal membership card, a free newsletter packed with recipes, competitions, bargain book offers, plus big cash savings.

**AND an Introductory FREE GIFT for YOU.
Turn over the page for details.**

Fill in and send this coupon back today
and we'll send you
4 Introductory
Doctor Nurse Romances yours to keep
FREE
At the same time we will reserve a
subscription to Mills & Boon
Doctor Nurse Romances for you. Every
two months you will receive the latest
8 new titles, delivered direct to your door.
You don't pay extra for delivery. Postage and
packing is always completely Free.
There is no obligation or commitment—
you receive books only for
as long as you want to.

It's easy! Fill in the coupon below and return it to
**MILLS & BOON READER SERVICE, FREEPOST, P.O. BOX 236,
CROYDON, SURREY CR9 9EL.**

Please note: READERS IN SOUTH AFRICA write to
Mills & Boon Ltd., Postbag X3010,
Randburg 2125, S. Africa.

- -

FREE BOOKS CERTIFICATE

**To: Mills & Boon Reader Service, FREEPOST, P.O. Box 236,
Croydon, Surrey CR9 9EL.**

Please send me, free and without obligation, four Dr. Nurse Romances, and reserve a
Reader Service Subscription for me. If I decide to subscribe I shall receive, following my free
parcel of books, eight new Dr. Nurse Romances every two months for £8.00, post and
packing free. If I decide not to subscribe, I shall write to you within 10 days. The free books
are mine to keep in any case. I understand that I may cancel my subscription at any time
simply by writing to you. I am over 18 years of age.
Please write in BLOCK CAPITALS.

Name _____

Address _____

_____

_____ Postcode _____

SEND NO MONEY — TAKE NO RISKS.

*Remember, postcodes speed delivery. Offer applies in UK only and is not valid to
present subscribers. Mills & Boon reserve the right to exercise discretion
in granting membership. If price changes are necessary you will be noti-
fied. Offer expires 31st December 1984.*

8DN

EP1